The H **Island**

Jean Bellamy

The Haunted Island

Jean Bellamy

Illustrations by Judith Fry

Collins

Marshall Pickering

First published in Great Britain in 1990 by Marshall Pickering

Copyright in text © 1990 Jean Bellamy
Copyright in illustrations © 1990 Judith Fry

Marshall Pickering is an imprint of the Collins Religious Division,
part of the Collins Publishing Group, 8 Grafton Street, London
W1X 3LA

British Library Cataloguing in Publication Data
Bellamy, Jean
   The Haunted Island.
   I. Title
   823'.914 [J]

   ISBN 0-7208-0753-0

Text set in Plantin by Avocet Robinson, Buckingham.
Printed and bound in Great Britain by
Cox and Wyman Ltd, Reading, Berks.

Contents

Chapter 1

The Island

The children stood on the cliff-top looking out across the bay. It was the first evening of the summer holidays and Nick and Meg had just arrived to spend a few weeks with their cousins at the MacLaren guest-house. They had watched the sun sink below the horizon like a great fiery ball; now dusk was falling, casting long grey shadows across the craggy cliffs, shrouding the bay in gloom.

'What's it called, Tessa?' asked fourteen-year-old Nick, staring intently towards the island lying some distance offshore.

'What's what called?' murmured Tessa vaguely, her mind on Badger the Welsh border collie who had gone missing.

'The island, of course!'

'Don't think it's got a name,' his thirteen-year-old cousin shrugged. She cupped her hands to her mouth again and shouted '*Badger!*' at the top of her voice.

'It's got to have a name!' Nick argued.

'Why's it got to have a name?' demanded ten-year-old Peter with a frown.

'All self-respecting islands have names, that's why,' Nick told him. Paula, Peter's twin, followed his gaze. 'Looks sort of spooky, doesn't it?' she murmured.

Nick ran his hands through his mop of tousled hair and snapped his fingers. 'That's it!' he shouted, 'the Haunted Island!'

There was a short pause, Tessa started to laugh, but his

sister Meg looked uneasy. 'Haunted, why haunted?' she asked.

'Because it's creepy, silly!' Nick told her. 'Any houses on it, Tess?'

'Only one old ruined cottage. Where on earth can Badger be?' she sighed, staring all round.

Nick wasn't interested in the fate of the collie, though. 'Someone must have lived there once then,' he persisted.

'A hermit, perhaps,' suggested auburn-haired Paula, eyeing her cousin with interest.

'A ghost more likely!' Peter said with a giggle.

'Why doesn't anyone live there now?' Nick demanded.

'Would you like to live in a ruin?' Tessa asked.

'Be all right in the summer. Might be a bit of a laugh!' Nick looked at the twins. 'Do people ever land there?'

'Sometimes, I s'pose! Dad's promised to take us in *Golden Spray* one day,' Peter volunteered. Nick wasn't listening though; with eyes half-closed he was trying to work out the distance between the island and the shore.

'Bet I could swim out to it!' he said at last.

There was a moment's startled silence; Peter was the first to speak. 'Bet you couldn't!' he retorted. 'It's miles!'

'About a mile, I'd say,' Nick said.

'You'd drown before you got half way!' Tessa told him scornfully.

Paula was beginning to tire of the subject. 'I wonder where Badger can be?' she mused, but Nick still wasn't listening.

'There's a line of rocks out there,' he said, gazing beyond the island to where a thin, foam-flecked ridge lay dimly visible.

'We call those the Deadmen's Teeth!' Paula told him, rolling her eyes.

'Why "Deadmen's Teeth"?' he frowned.

'Ships have gone down on that reef, thousands of 'em!' Peter explained.

'On the whirligigs!' put in Paula.

'She means whirlpools,' Tessa translated.

Nick snorted and fell about laughing; Meg didn't think

2

it funny though. She stared fearfully towards the long black outline fast merging with the shadows, then looked at Tessa. 'What can have happened to Badger?' she said, changing the subject.

'Let's all shout together!' her cousin suggested. So they all yelled 'Badger!' at the top of their voices.

'Ssh!' Nick said suddenly and they held their breath and listened; from a little way out in the bay came the faint creak of oars. Nick strained his eyes into the darkness. 'There's someone out there in a rowing-boat!' he breathed.

'That'll be old Bill getting in his lobster-pots,' Tessa said matter-of-factly. She jerked her head over to the left. 'He lives in a cottage just above Kennet Sands.'

'Lobster pots!' Meg exclaimed. 'What are they?'

'Things they catch lobsters in,' Paula explained.

They listened again; this time the plop-plop of oars was clearly audible. Minutes later they heard the scrunch of footsteps on the shingle somewhere over to their right. 'Bill's come in on this side tonight,' Tessa said. 'I wonder why?'

'Perhaps it isn't Bill,' Nick murmured mysteriously.

'Can you eat lobsters?' Meg wanted to know.

'Course, they're smashing!' Tessa said. She started calling Badger again and at that moment they heard something that sounded like a shower of small stones falling down the cliff face. It was followed by a soft pad-pad on the narrow track leading up from the beach close to where they stood; next minute a dark shape launched itself into view. As it reached the top with a bound, Tessa drew a long breath of relief. It was the collie!

'Good old Badger!' she gasped, throwing herself eagerly at her pet. 'You don't half seem pleased with yourself. What have you been up to?'

He stood wagging his tail, tongue lolling out.

'Where *have* you been, you naughty boy?' Paula asked.

'Hey!' Nick shouted. 'He's got something in his mouth!'

Tessa squatted down for a closer inspection. 'So he has! What have you brought us, Badger?'

'It's a mouse!' Paula shouted.

'So it is!' yelled her twin bouncing excitedly up and down. Meg turned a shade pale, however, and backed away. Nick stooped and tried to take the dead creature from between the dog's sharp white teeth. Badger growled warningly.

'Serve him right if he bit him,' Peter muttered to Paula out of the corner of his mouth.

'Don't tease him!' Tessa warned, then looked at her watch. 'Come on everybody. Mum said we were to be in by half past nine and it's nearly ten!' Calling to Badger, she set off at a trot along the winding cliff path in the direction of the village; Meg followed a close second, the collie bounding at her heels. The twins tagged on behind shouting, 'Good oh! Cocoa time!'

Only Nick remained, in no hurry to go; out to sea the island had become a dark blur against the horizon. As he stood meditating he was suddenly aware of a tall figure looming up out of the darkness. It passed him on the cliff path and walked on in the direction of Kennet Sands. Nick got the impression of someone a bit older than himself with a mop of straw-coloured hair, wearing a white sweater and khaki shorts.

Meg returned at that moment and when Nick looked again the stranger had vanished.

'Come on, Nick!' his sister urged. 'I want my supper.'

'OK – no hurry,' he told her.

They left the cliff path and joined the road that led back to the village. Nick looked ahead to his cousins, fast disappearing up the hill; there was a thoughtful expression in his eyes.

'What do you think of them?' Meg enquired apprehensively.

'Things are going to need livening up around here,' he said with a wink.

Meg shrugged. 'We don't really know them yet, do we?'

'Things are going to need livening up!' he said with a wink.

4

She gave him an anxious look. 'How?' she asked.

He changed the subject. 'What about a walk before breakfast tomorrow morning?' he suggested.

Tessa called to them at that moment and they quickened their pace up the hill. The guest-house stood at the top on the right-hand side; it was large with white gates. When they arrived they found that Uncle Bob had just got back from a day's fishing. He greeted them warmly. 'Welcome to Cornwall, both of you!' he said cheerfully. 'How you've both shot up since we last saw you. It must be six years!'

Aunt Jane appeared at that moment. 'You're back then! Supper's ready, you must be starving!'

Tessa led the way along the passage to a little room off the kitchen. There were mugs of steaming hot chocolate and crab sandwiches on the table, along with cake and biscuits. 'They'll be fine after a good night's sleep,' Jane MacLaren told her husband. 'Tuck in all of you!'

'What are we going to do tomorrow?' Nick asked as they sipped their drinks and sampled the food.

'Anything you like, within reason!' his uncle told him.

'Can we go skin-diving and looking for wrecks?'

'Not much chance of that, I'm afraid! We leave that to the experts!'

'Can we swim down at Sandy Cove, Auntie?' Meg asked.

'If you're careful and don't go out too far!'

Meg glanced at Nick but his thoughts were elsewhere. 'What's the name of the island?' he asked casually.

'Which island?' asked his uncle.

There was a short pause.

'The one opposite Sandy Cove,' Tessa explained. 'Nick's taken a fancy to it!'

'The locals just call it Whale Island,' his uncle told him.

'Could we go over there with the youth club and have a picnic, Dad?' Tessa suggested.

The twins eyes sparkled. 'Great!' they agreed. None of the children had been over to the island yet.

There was a pause. Nick eyed Meg warily. 'What's the youth club?' he asked.

'It's to do with the church,' Tessa explained.

Nick glanced at his sister again when he thought it was safe to do so.

'What sort of things do you do?' Meg wanted to know.

'Barbecues, beach games — all sorts of things!' her uncle told her. 'We get about forty youngsters along, all ages.' He looked at Tessa and added, 'That's a good suggestion of yours about the island. I'll get it organised.'

They finished their meal. 'We're full up at the guest-house, I'm afraid,' Aunt Jane said as they got up from the table. 'Tessa's sleeping round at Martha Pengelly's cottage two doors down and we're boarding Nick and Meg next door with the Trembaths. You'll have all your meals here, of course.'

Nick caught his sister's eye. It was the best piece of news he'd heard so far; they'd have a bit more freedom sleeping out. Meg felt uneasy, though. What was her brother planning? she asked herself. Tessa broke into her thoughts.

'I'll show you your rooms,' she volunteered. 'Dad will carry your luggage round.'

They said goodnight to their aunt who was busy at the sink with an enormous pile of washing-up. 'See you in the morning, dears!' she told them. 'Sleep well!'

'Good night, Auntie!' said Meg, coming over a bit homesick; then she and Nick went next door with Tessa.

Both their rooms were large and light with crisp muslin curtains at the windows. Nick's faced out over the bay whilst Meg's looked inland across fields of yellow corn stretching away into the distance.

'Don't forget, we're getting up early tomorrow to go for a walk!' Nick reminded his sister when Tessa had gone. 'About half past six.'

'All right!' she yawned without much enthusiasm. 'If I'm awake!'

'You'd better be!' he told her. 'I'll set my alarm.'

They said goodnight and went to their rooms. Meg was

soon in bed and asleep but Nick stayed staring out of the window for a while. It was very quiet; only the distant lap of the water on the shore and the occasional cry of a seabird broke the silence. After the noise of the city, the stillness was so intense, he felt he could almost put out his hand and touch it.

Across the bay the faint outline of the island was still visible, though the reef had completely merged with the shadows. As he stood looking out into the night it seemed to Nick that the island beckoned.

Chapter 2
Chris

Nick woke at six next morning, brought to earth by the strident ringing of the alarm bell. He was soon up and dressed and in a few minutes a yawning Meg joined him on the landing.

'Ssh, follow me and don't make a noise!' he whispered.

'Where are we going?' Meg asked nervously with a quick look towards the other two bedrooms.

'You'll see when we get there!' he hissed, tip-toeing towards the top of the stairs.

They crept silently down into the hall; Nick turned the key in the lock of the front door and they went quietly down the path towards the gate. Meg heaved a sigh of relief as they walked rapidly away down the hill in the same direction they had taken the previous evening.

'Great!' said Nick catching a glimpse of the sea stretching away like a sheet of glass to the horizon. Already the sun was coming up, giving promise of a fine day.

'Do you think the tide's coming in or going out?' Meg asked as they turned on to the cliff path.

'I dunno! Coming in, I should think. It won't be high tide yet – not for ages!'

In a few minutes they drew level with the track up which Badger had come the previous evening. They ran helter-skelter down to the beach and there was a look of keen anticipation on Nick's face as he stared seawards. Meg followed his gaze to where the island floated in the pale haze of early dawn. It appeared a lot more inviting by daylight, she had to admit. Busy with his thoughts, Nick turned to his sister, an eager expression on his face.

'I reckon I *could* swim out there,' he told her, a glint in his eye.

She looked at him aghast. 'You'd never make it!'

'A piece of cake!' he said.

'You heard what they said last night about it being dangerous!'

'I don't care what they said; they were only trying to put the frighteners on us!' He picked up a pebble and hurled it out over the water, trying to make it bounce. 'Don't forget – I got the prize for swimming last term, Meg. Half a mile!'

'That was in the baths! It's different in the sea!'

'Rubbish! You can look after my clothes whilst I'm gone.'

'Someone will see us!'

'Not at the time we're going . . . Come on, let's go and see what's round the corner!'

It was useless arguing; Meg knew her brother too well. They walked the length of the beach which was little more than a small cove, then round to the next bay which was bigger. Nick looked for the island but it was no longer visible.

'I'm hungry!' he announced when they had gone about half-way. 'Let's go back!'

They retraced their steps, scrambled up the cliff path, and made their way back to the guest-house. Tessa and the twins were already sitting down to breakfast when they walked into the little dining-room where the family had their meals.

'Hello there! We're just talking about the barbecue this evening,' Tessa greeted them. 'It's being held at Kennet Sands, the next beach along from Sandy Bay.'

'We had one last Saturday and it was great!' Peter said.

Nick rolled expressive eyes at Meg when he thought no one was looking. He didn't like the sound of it at all. Bob MacLaren appeared at that moment with a packet of green cards in his hand.

'Hello, Nick! Hello, Meg! Sleep well?' He looked at Tessa. 'I've had the programme of events printed for the youth club, including Saturday's barbecue,' he told her. 'Who's going to volunteer to take them round?'

'Meg and I could do the ones around here,' Tessa suggested. 'Nick and the twins can do the camp-site.'

Her mother came in with the toast at that moment. 'The camp-site's full, by all accounts,' she told them. 'The scouts have just arrived.'

'What do we have to do?' Meg asked warily, wishing she hadn't got to be involved.

'Just give the cards out to anyone who's interested.'

Nick shrugged resignedly. 'That's easy enough, I suppose. After that can we have a swim and go exploring?'

'Yes, Kennet Sands are quite safe. Sandy Bay's all right so long as you don't go too far out,' his uncle told him.

Meg looked at Nick but he avoided her eyes.

They finished breakfast and Tessa and Meg helped to clear away.

'Come on, let's get the tickets organised,' Nick told the twins, anxious to get the job over and done with. 'Half for us, half for Tessa and Meg.'

They divided them up, then set off in the direction of the village, Badger in tow. They hadn't gone far when Tessa called a halt. 'This is where we part company,' she said, 'Meg and I will do the cottages and bungalows around here. The twins will show you where the camp-site is, Nick. See you later at Sandy Bay!'

Meg would rather have gone with her brother but there was nothing she could do about it; her cousin had it all arranged. Badger looked as though he would have liked to cut himself in two but finally opted to go with Nick and the twins. With a last look at her brother, Meg turned off to the left with Tessa.

The others continued straight on. 'This is where we turn off,' Peter said after about five minutes. They went right into a narrow lane and presently a big field lay ahead with what looked like hundreds of tents. There seemed to be a lot of activity going on.

They walked in through the gate and Nick looked around. There were a number of visitors' tents at the near end; further afield the scouts were busy getting ready for a day's hike, putting on stout walking boots and filling their rucksacks with provisions. Peter had the cards and he thrust some into Nick's hand.

'You do that side, Paula and I will do this!'

Nick frowned; he didn't much appreciate being ordered about by this cocky ten-year-old. There was nothing to be gained by arguing, however, so he took them with a muttered 'Thanks!' and mooched off between the long line of tents. Families were sitting on tarpaulins on the ground eating their breakfasts; there were a number of youngsters around, most of them shouting and yelling their heads off. Some of the kids looked interested when Nick thrust a programme into their hands; others just stared and he felt a bit of a prune.

On the other side of the field, Peter and Paula had no such inhibitions however; they were enjoying themselves! They ran up to the far end and got rid of a lot of invitations amongst the scouts, then they came back. Outside a bright orange tent a boy of about their own age was flying an enormous kite. It twisted and turned as though it were alive, soaring higher and higher into the blue arc of the sky. They left an invitation with his parents, then looked round. Someone was standing outside a small brown tent pitched slightly apart from the others close to the hedge. He appeared to be putting film into a camera and there were some papers scattered on the ground at his feet. He scooped them up and stuffed them into the pocket of his jeans when he saw the twins.

'Hello!' Peter said. 'We're Peter and Paula! Would you like to come to a beach barbecue next Saturday evening at Kennet Sands?'

'What's it to do with?'

'Church youth club!' Paula told him, handing him a programme. 'It's all about it on there!'

Someone was standing outside a small brown tent

He looked at the card and there was a short silence.

'What's your name?' Peter enquired.

'Er . . . Chris!'

At that moment Nick strolled over.

'This is Chris!' Peter introduced. 'Nick's our cousin and he's staying with us.'

'Hi!' Nick said and gave him a casual glance. He was about seventeen, tall and lean with a thatch of blond hair; he wore khaki shorts and a white sweater. There was something vaguely familiar about him, Nick thought. Where had he seen him before? he asked himself, and wracked his brains to remember.

Chris studied the invitation card. 'Can't promise, I'll have to think about it,' he said, looking at the twins.

'We're going over to the island soon!' Paula volunteered.

There was another silence. Nick glanced at Chris; a peculiar expression seemed to have crept into his eyes. 'The one they call Whale Island,' Nick said.

'I didn't know people landed there.'

'You can if you've got your own boat,' Peter told him. 'We're all going over there in our Dad's launch. She's called *Golden Spray*.'

'When?' Chris asked, looking at the invitation again.

'It's not been decided when yet, that's why it's not down there,' Paula explained.

'We could let you know,' Peter said.

'Will you be coming to the barbecue?' Paula asked.

'Can't promise! I'll – er – think about it.' Chris turned towards his tent; the interview was obviously at an end as far as he was concerned. Peter and Paula called out 'goodbye' and Nick moved thoughtfully away.

They did the remainder of the tents together, Badger scampering around after rabbits. Then they made their way to Sandy Bay.

Tessa and Meg were waiting for them at the bottom of the cliff path when they arrived. Nick noticed that there was a lot more beach showing than there had been before breakfast; the sea was running out quite quickly leaving a wide band of gleaming wet sand in its wake. A gull with snow-white feathers and a yellow beak and legs stood on a rock screeching noisily.

'Thought you said the tide was coming in!' Meg shouted to her brother as soon as she saw him.

'It's been in and it's going out again.' Tessa explained. 'You have to make sure you know which it's doing. I got cut off once and had to climb the cliff!'

'How awful!' Meg said with a shiver. 'What happened?'

'A boat came and rescued me! I'll tell you about it sometime,' she promised.

Nick, busy with his thoughts once more, was only half listening. He stared towards the island again; it looked quite welcoming with the sun shimmering on it. Even the ragged outline of the reef beyond seemed less menacing in the light of day. He thought of the chap they had just met up at the camp-site and wondered again where he had seen him. There was something a bit mysterious about him, he decided. Chris had seemed interested in the island too, and he wondered why . . .

Then suddenly it came to him – it had been last night, of course! He'd been standing on the cliff-top on his own after the others had gone on. A tall figure had loomed up out of the darkness and passed him on the cliff path . . . At the same time Nick remembered the boat they had heard out in the bay, the one Tessa had said was probably old Bill's. Nick had an idea she had been mistaken . . .

Badger appeared at that moment, interrupting his train of thought. The collie had a stick in his mouth and Nick forgot about Chris and the island for the moment.

'He wants a game!' Peter said and Nick picked up a pebble and hurled it towards the sea. Badger ran straight in after it.

'Isn't he clever!' Paula said. 'He can swim!'

'All dogs can swim!' Nick said scornfully. He looked at Badger as he paddled round and round in circles searching in vain for the stone.

14

'He'll never find it!' Peter pouted. 'It's not fair teasing him!'

Nick just laughed and chucked another. Badger disappeared beneath the water several times. He came up at last with something in his mouth and started swimming towards the shore.

'Bet that's not the one I threw!' Nick said.

'He's found one anyway,' Tessa told him. 'Good old Badger! Give it me!'

The collie laid it at her feet and she found a small piece of driftwood. She threw it and watched him go after the stick which floated on the top of the water.

Nick soon lost interest in the dog.

'I'm going swimming!' he said.

He changed quickly, plunged into the sea, and struck out for some nearby rocks.

Chapter 3
The Barbecue

The next few days passed uneventfully. The children swam and explored the beaches and to Meg's relief Nick said no more about swimming to the island.

'Would you like to go rowing?' Tessa asked her cousins at breakfast one morning.

They all thought it a good idea and as soon as they had finished eating the five of them and Badger set off for the quay where she kept her boat. *Puffin* was at the bottom of the harbour steps when they got there, rocking gently at anchor. She was blue with the name painted on her side in large white lettering. Tessa got in first to hold her steady, Nick, Meg and the twins followed and Badger came last, leaping from several steps up and nearly tipping them all into the water. When everybody was settled, Tessa rowed them out as far as the gap in the harbour wall.

'Can I have a go?' Nick kept pestering her, but Tessa didn't seem keen on the idea.

'Have you ever rowed before?' she asked dubiously.

'No, but any idiot could, I should think!' he told her. She shrugged. 'All right, in a minute. When we get to the inner harbour.' She turned the boat round and started rowing back; it was peaceful and quiet on the water, Meg thought. 'You'll have to be careful when we change places,' Tessa warned, 'otherwise you'll have us all in.'

'Whoopee!' Peter shouted, but Paula pulled a face and Meg stared down at the bed of the ocean several yards below. Tessa manoeuvred between a tall white yacht and a fishing smack as they entered the smaller harbour, then she looked at Nick.

'OK,' she said. 'I'll go this side, you go that. The boat has to be balanced, you see, otherwise we'll capsize.'

They both stood up and *Puffin* rocked precariously.

'Help,' Paula giggled, but the change-over took place without mishap. Nick grasped the oars and started to row. A lot of sea-water came flying over amidships.

'Hey, you're shipping crabs!' Peter protested and Paula sniggered with laughter.

Meg wasn't amused however. 'Oh Nick, do be careful!' she wailed. 'I'm sodden!'

'Feather your oars!' Tessa said and Nick looked blank. 'Keep them nearer the surface. It's easier that way.' she explained.

Nick puffed and blew as he tried to follow her instructions. He soon got the hang of it though; he was doing quite well now and enjoying himself. The dinghy shifted through the water apace and in no time they were back at the harbour steps.

'Not bad for a first go!' Tessa admitted as he drew in his oars. *Puffin* bumped against a rock at that moment, however, and everyone shouted with laughter. Paula stood up ready to get off, and as she did so glanced up towards the top of the quay.

'There's old Bill up there!' she announced and Peter followed her gaze.

'He's talking to that chap from the camp-site,' he observed.

Nick, still grappling with the oars, glanced up quickly. At the same time Chris looked down into the boat and saw him. Their eyes met.

Puffin lurched against the steps and Tessa jumped up. She leant out and secured the mooring-rope to a rusty ring in the harbour wall; they all got out and scrambled up on to the steep seaweed-covered steps. When they reached the top of the jetty Nick stared swiftly round. There was only old Bill leaning on the harbour wall, though; Chris had disappeared.

★   ★   ★

The next day was Saturday. The barbecue was to be held on Kennet Sands, the next beach round the corner from Sandy Bay. The youth club nearly always had it to themselves so there was plenty of room to spread out. Tessa, the twins and Badger set out as soon as tea was over for there was a lot to be done. Nick and Meg had gone off on their own after lunch and hadn't been seen since. Tessa hoped they would remember about the beach party and turn up later.

Tessa's father had left home even earlier and preparations were already well under way when the three children arrived. Steve the youth-club leader was there, too, and David from the coastguard station with his dog Sheba. They were building an enormous bonfire up towards the top of the beach, out of reach of the tide.

'See if you can find more sticks and things whilst I help Mum,' Tessa told the twins to keep them out of mischief. 'There should be lots lying around after that bit of a storm the other night.'

Peter and Paula did as they were told; they liked collecting driftwood. They ran off across the wide stretch of sand towards the tideline and were soon back with their arms full. Meanwhile Tessa helped to unload the food from the Land-Rover parked on top of the low cliff. By the time everything was unpacked, children were rolling up in groups of threes and fours, coming from the direction of the village. Tessa recognised her friend Melanie and waved. Gary Travers and his pals were there, she noticed, and there were some scouts and quite a lot of other youngsters whom she hadn't seen before. Dad's invitation cards had obviously paid off!

By the time seven o' clock arrived the beach was quite crowded and the bonfire was ready to be lit. Someone put

By the time seven o'clock arrived the beach was quite crowded

a match to it and bright orange flames licked around the dry crackling wood. Soon sausages were sizzling merrily on the spit.

'Hot dogs!' shouted Steve and David, ready with the bread rolls. 'Anyone for hot dogs!'

The kids didn't need to be told twice; they surged forward to form a long queue. Crisp, crusty rolls were doled out filled with fried onions and a sausage apiece.

'Scrumptious!' Melanie said, her mouth full.

'Always tastes better out of doors!' Tessa agreed.

Buns, cake and biscuits, fresh fruit salad and cream followed, along with squash and Coke. In the midst of it all, Tessa looked towards the cliff and caught sight of Meg and Nick hurrying along the path. They came down on to the beach and headed straight towards the food.

'Thought that would bring them along!' Tessa commented. 'Hello there, you're too late!' she shouted. 'We've eaten it all!'

They looked shattered until they realised she was only joking. 'Saved some especially for you!' Melanie told them.

'I'm starving!' Nick announced, and Aunt Jane overheard. 'It's all that sea air!' she told him.

'It seems ages since lunch time,' he complained, and Meg admitted that they'd only had enough money for a bar of chocolate between them; all the rest had gone on ice-cream and fizzy lemonade. Tessa whispered to Melanie that if they must stay out and miss tea, what could they expect?

Nick demolished two hot dogs and a lot of other goodies besides, then he looked seawards hoping to catch a glimpse of Whale Island. They were a bit further along the coast here at Kennet Sands though, and it was just out of sight around the corner.

'Let's go and look at that cave over there!' he suggested to Meg when they had finished eating. He didn't say so to her but he had an idea he'd be able to see the island from that vantage point.

They wandered across the sand towards the right side

of the bay. The cliffs rose a lot higher at this end of the beach than the other; a large black aperture confronted them which seemed to extend a long way back. They stepped inside and the sand felt dank and cold under their bare feet. Water plopped on to their heads from the roof and the further they walked into the interior the chillier it became. Meg shivered, partly from cold, partly from fear; she didn't much like it inside the cave, though Nick thought it was great. He'd been right about the island too, he soon discovered; it was just visible from the entrance.

'Come on, let's get back!' Meg pleaded as the cave became narrower and narrower and finally petered out altogether. They turned round and made for the entrance. Meg heaved a sigh of relief as they stepped out on to the warm sand; it was good to be out in the sunshine again.

'Wonder if Chris is here,' Nick murmured as they strolled back towards the others.

'Who's Chris?' Meg asked with a frown.

'Oh, just a chap I met up at the camp-site,' he told her casually. He looked around but there was no one resembling the lone camper. Instead his eye alighted on a small gang of boys arguing on the outskirts of the crowd. A piping voice wafted over to them.

'Our Dad took us out fishing today. I caught one as big as that!' A freckle-faced youth of about eleven extended his arms to indicate something the size of a small whale.

'You never!' Gary protested, getting ready to do battle.

'That's nothing, Gary Travers!' scoffed another of the group. 'I caught half-a-dozen that size the other day!'

'You're fibbing!' Gary protested. He levelled his fists and glared at his opponent, obviously spoiling for a fight.

Nick glanced at Meg and winked. 'Must have been a whale!' he said loudly, and hearing him, Gary's head shot round.

'You keep out of this!' he warned belligerently, then looked at Nick and Meg more closely. 'What *you* two doing here anyway?' he went on. 'This is for club members only!'

Nick's hackles rose. 'We've got as much right to be here as anyone! What *you* doing here, more like!' he added sarcastically. 'Thought this was supposed to be a Sunday School party!'

A gale of laughter greeted this remark. At that moment Steve strode up. The youth-club leader was big and brawny and he went over and had a word or two with the lads. They slouched off to the other side of the beach and Steve turned to Nick and Meg.

'Sorry about that!' he told them.

'That's sorted them out anyway!' Nick grinned.

Tessa and Melanie joined them at that moment. 'They're always stirring it up!' Tessa said. 'They spoil everybody's fun!'

'We don't want to ban them entirely – if it can be avoided,' Steve said. 'You never know, they may improve!'

'The best thing is – don't get involved,' Bob MacLaren advised, overhearing.

Remembering Nick's provocative remark, Meg glanced at her brother. 'Can we go fishing some time, Uncle?' she asked, changing the subject.

He nodded. 'Of course! Next week, if you like,' he promised.

'What do you catch?' she asked.

'Whales!' Nick butted in with a grin, and Meg bit her lip.

'Mackerel, mostly,' her uncle said. 'We take them home and cook them for supper. Nothing like fresh mackerel in my opinion!'

Peter and Paula, standing near, caught the fag end of the conversation. 'We going fishing again soon, Dad?' Peter asked.

'If you behave yourselves!' he teased.

'I love mackerel!' Paula said. 'It's gorgeous with lots of lemon squeezed all over it!'

A game of cricket followed and Nick found himself fielding next to Gary Travers. He carefully avoided his eye, however, for he had decided to take his uncle's advice and not get himself involved – for this evening at any rate. Every now and then he glanced towards the far right-hand corner of the bay where the island lay out to sea just out of sight around the corner. He had other and more interesting matters on his mind at the moment . . .

*　　*　　*

As soon as the game was over everyone ran down to the sea to cool off. Nick and Meg stayed in longer than most of the others; sea-bathing was a novelty for them and they thought it great – much better than the baths. The ocean was very flat and calm but Uncle Bob had promised to take them to a beach where they could do some surfing sometime.

'It's not been so bad after all, has it?' Meg said to her brother as they came out of the water. 'Do you think we go home now?' she asked.

'No such luck, I'm afraid! There's the epilogue or whatever they call it first, remember!'

The tide was coming in quite fast, running swiftly over the smooth sand, trickling into the holes the youngsters had dug. They looked over to where Uncle Bob, Steve and some of the others were fanning the dying embers of the bonfire. The children were beginning to drift back; some were already sitting around the fire and Tessa and Melanie were giving out books. Nick sighed, a restless look in his eyes. 'Do you think we can slip away?' he muttered.

Meg looked towards the cliff path; it was in full view of the beach. 'Not now, we can't,' she told him. 'It's too late – they'd see us.' She gave her brother a quick sideways glance; he'd been unusually quiet and brooding all afternoon, he'd got something on his mind she was sure. At that moment there flashed into her head what he had said about swimming out to the island. He hadn't

23

mentioned it again since the beginning of the holiday but she felt suddenly uneasy . . .

She found her clothes and dressed quickly, then walked over to join the others. Her brother was already there, sitting on his own, well to the back of the crowd. Dusk was falling; the bonfire was beginning to splutter into life again.

'Have a song-book!' Tessa said, tossing a couple over for Nick and herself. As Meg idly turned the pages, she found her thoughts travelling back over the last few days. So far the holiday had been much more fun than she'd expected. Tessa hadn't bothered them much and they'd been allowed to go off by themselves and do their own thing. In spite of it all she was beginning to enjoy Cornwall; it was a world apart from the hot dusty streets of the city back home.

Steve stood up at that moment to make a few announcements. The one about the island trip the following afternoon caught Meg's attention; she found herself quite looking forward to it. When she looked at Nick, however, she saw that he was miles away, tracing patterns in the sand with his forefinger. He kept his mouth firmly closed during the singing of the hymn that followed.

The youth leader was on his feet again. He was talking about God; he spoke about Him as though he knew Him personally. 'God is everywhere,' he said, and Nick stopped doodling and looked thoughtful. He wasn't sure that God even existed, but he found himself listening, all the same. 'God is all-seeing, too,' Steve went on. 'He knows our thoughts, our plans, our intentions . . .'

Nick wriggled uncomfortably at this and when the speaker continued, 'God is interested in each one of us! He asks that we give our lives in his service!' he switched off altogether. His life was his own, he told himself, to do what he wanted with. He fidgeted and looked at Meg; she appeared to be listening with rapt attention.

The bonfire crackled and glowed, emitting a shower of sparks; the sea was running in quite close now; dusk was falling, casting long grey shadows across the beach. It was cosy and friendly around the bonfire, Meg thought. She remembered what Steve had just said about God being everywhere – the idea was comforting somehow . . . She looked at Nick again and her fears came rushing back. He had something on his mind this evening, she was certain.

There was a short prayer, then the usual buzz of conversation broke out, Tessa, Melanie and some of the others ran around collecting up the song-books.

Nick jumped to his feet. 'That's that over then!' he breathed.

'Now we can go home!' Meg said a little too eagerly.

Nick shook his head.

'We're not going home – yet!' he told her firmly.

*   *   *

It took a little while to pack everything up; the girls helped to carry the remains of the feast back to the Land-Rover whilst the boys had fun dousing the bonfire. Tired but happy the children sang out their goodbyes and set off along the cliff path for home. When the last of them had gone and everything had been stowed away, the MacLarens looked around for Nick and Meg, whom they had temporarily forgotten about in the confusion. Melanie said that she had seen them leave the beach ten minutes earlier, heading back along the cliff in the direction of home.

'They're probably back by now,' Bob MacLaren said.

'Wish they were a bit more friendly,' Tessa remarked as she climbed into the back of the Land-Rover behind her father.

'Give them time,' her mother advised. 'They'll settle down.'

The twins and Melanie piled in beside Tessa, and Bob MacLaren steered a path over the rough uneven ground. They bumped their way along the dusty rutted track towards the road and were soon home. Tessa went into the guest-house for a cup of Horlicks before going to the cottage. There was still no sign of Nick and Meg.

'I'll go next door and see if they're back,' she told her parents as she finished her drink. There was no one there, however – the Trembaths were out; so she decided to go along to the café down the road before going to bed. Her cousins went there for a milk-shake last thing some evenings.

They weren't there, though. 'I'll keep a look out for them from my window,' she told herself as she walked up the path to the cottage. She was just going up the stairs when Martha Pengelly beckoned her eagerly into the kitchen.

'Come and see what's here!' she invited.

Full of curiosity, Tessa retraced her steps and found the old lady bending over a cardboard box in the corner of the room. Inside six little balls of black fluff were huddled helplessly together, their eyes tightly closed. Martha's black cat, Flossie, stood proudly by, having just presented her mistress with a litter of kittens!

Tessa was enchanted with the tiny helpless creatures and when at last she tore herself away she had completely forgotten about Nick and Meg. She was soon in bed, and not long afterwards Martha bolted the front door and came slowly up the stairs. Tessa fell into a light sleep, to awaken some time later to the sound of the grandfather clock in the hall below. She counted the strokes and as the last one died away, realised with surprise that it had chimed eleven. She had been asleep only just over an hour, so what had disturbed her?

She stared at the ceiling, wider awake now, and at that moment there came a sound like a shower of small pebbles spattering against glass. She held her breath, looking with a puzzled frown towards the blue check curtains drawn across the little attic window; then, coming fully awake, she jumped quickly out of bed and sped across the linoleum. As she pulled the curtains aside, the sound came again. She looked down into the little back garden and became aware of a figure standing on the small square front lawn with its neat border of flowers. In that split second of time she remembered her cousins!

As Tessa gazed down at the pale, terrified face raised to the window she knew at once that it was Meg. A thrill of alarm ran through her and she bit her lip. What had happened, and where was Nick? she asked herself.

Chapter 4
Nick in Trouble

Tessa was just about to push up the window and call out when she changed her mind. Meg looked in a terrible state; she'd better get down to her straight away, she told herself. Her heart went bumpety-bump as she pulled on her clothes and grabbed up her anorak. Then with her sandals dangling from her hand, she eased open the bedroom door and crept barefoot on to the landing.

The treads creaked noisily as she trod stealthily down the stairs. Would Martha wake up and hear her? she wondered anxiously. No sound came from the bedroom on the other side of the landing however, and in a few seconds she had opened the front door and was outside on the gravel path, face to face with Meg. Her cousin looked an awful sight: her short, curly hair was plastered to her head, her face streaked with dirt. Red eyes swollen with crying, sodden shirt and denims from which the water ran off in rivulets on to the path, completed the picture.

'What's happened? Where's Nick?' Tessa hissed in a loud whisper. Meg didn't answer and Tessa stared at her with growing alarm. Her tears showed no signs of lessening so she grabbed her arm impatiently.

'What's happened, Meg, for goodness' sake?' she repeated urgently.

Great shuddering gasps shook her cousin from head to toe. 'W-we w-went for a sw-swim b-by moonlight. N-Nick wanted to swim out to the i-island . . . I t-told him n-not to,' she blubbered.

'Swim out to the island!' Tessa almost shouted. 'He

Her cousin looked an awful sight

hasn't tried to swim out to the island!'

'I-I tried to stop him b-but he w-wouldn't listen t-to me!'

'He's an absolute idiot! Where is he now, for goodness' sake?'

'I . . . I d-don't know!' Meg quavered. 'He d-didn't c-come back! . . .'

'You're both crazy!' Tessa said horrified.

'I'm s-sorry, T-Tessa!'

'It's a bit late to be sorry, isn't it?'

Meg shook her head hopelessly. 'Wh-what are we going to do?' she breathed.

This was a good question, and Tessa took a grip of herself. The island was at least three-quarters of a mile from the shore; at high tide as it was now it would be about a mile. There were currents too, out there – dangerous ones; and the water would be icy cold at this time of the evening. Nobody but the strongest of swimmers – or a fool – would try swimming out to the island . . . Had he landed on one of the small rocks dotted around the bay? she asked herself. It was his only hope . . .

Meg broke in on her thoughts. 'D-do you think he-he got there, Tessa? . . . It was g-getting dark and I c-couldn't see . . . He's a good swimmer, he might have done!'

Tessa looked scornful. 'He'd need to be to swim out to the island, the stupid boy!' she stormed – for even if you came from Birmingham you should know better than to try swimming out there!

Now was no time for lecturing though, as well she knew. 'Come on, let's get down there!' she said and caught Meg's arm again. Next minute the two girls were out of the gate and racing down the road towards the beach.

It was a starlit night and the fields stretched gently away to the distant moor. In a nearby wood an owl hooted and from not far away came the murmur of the tide on the sea-shore. There was no one about; most people would be in bed and asleep by now. Tessa could hear her cousin's sniffs as she thudded along the road behind her. It occurred to her then that she hadn't asked a vital question.

'How long's he been gone?' she called out over her shoulder.

'A-about thr-three-quarters of an hour!' Meg wailed.

'Three-quarters of an hour!' Tessa echoed, aghast.

'I w-waited and waited and called . . .'

Tessa drew in her breath; in that time anything could have happened! Should she go back and fetch her father, she asked herself? Every second seemed vital though, and she stumbled blindly on down the hill towards the beach.

'Please God, help us to find Nick!' she breathed. 'Don't let it be too late!'

Meg tripped at that moment and would have gone sprawling if Tessa hadn't put out a steadying hand. They were on the top of the cliff now and out to sea lay the island, dimly visible in the semi-darkness. Their breath coming in gasps, the two girls sped along the cliff path and hurled themselves down the narrow track towards the deserted beach.

Tessa was the first to reach the bottom. Her eyes went straight to the little pile of clothing in the middle of the sand; then she gazed fearfully across the murky sea to the island, black and mysterious in the half-light. Not so far out now as it would have been three-quarters of an hour ago though, as she knew only too well! She gulped, forcing her eyes back to her cousin's anguished face.

'What are we going to do?' Meg sobbed hysterically, and even as she asked the question, Tessa came to a sudden decision.

'We'll have to row out in old Bill's dinghy. It's in the sand-dunes,' she said. They were off again over the wet sand, their flying feet scarcely touching it. 'Bill won't mind,' Tessa explained as they sped along. 'He . . . he lets me . . . use the boat . . . if mine's over at the harbour.'

They rounded the corner to the next beach and slipped and slithered their way over the wet rocks. Tessa raced on towards the dunes, darting over to the spot where the dinghy nestled in a hollow. The little boat was white, with 'Seagull' painted on her side in large black lettering. She

31

picked up the mooring rope and hitched it over her shoulder.

'Come on, Meg, give me a hand!' she ordered, and her cousin obeyed; then they were on their way towards the tide-line, pulling and pushing the boat between them.

It was hard going but they got there at last and Tessa rolled up her trouser legs and waded straight in amongst the thick fronds of seaweed and bladderwrack. A faint breeze ruffled the surface of the ocean as she guided the little craft into deeper water; as soon as it was afloat she jumped aboard. Meg followed, shivering, and Tessa took off her anorak and threw it to her. Then she sat down and fitted the oars expertly into the rowlocks on the gunwale. When Meg too was seated, she started to row and they were away.

Neither girl spoke. Only the creak of wood against wood and the faint splash splash of the blades as they flashed in and out of the water broke the silence. Tessa bent backwards and forwards to the rhythm of the oars; Meg sat hunched in the stern, bleak despair written all over her face as she stared terrified across the still, silent ocean.

Now and again they passed a solitary rock sticking up like a decayed black tooth out of the gleaming water. Tessa scanned each one as they passed, her only hope being that Nick had managed to reach one and cling on to it. There was no sign of life though, and an awful fear gripped her. Then she remembered the story they had heard in church last Sunday.

It had been the one about Jesus walking on the water. His disciples were out in their boat on the Lake of Galilee, crossing from one side to the other. It had been calm when they set out, but a storm had sprung up suddenly, as storms often do on Galilee. Rowing hard and getting nowhere they had panicked. Then Jesus had appeared, walking on the water. 'Be still!' he told the waves, and immediately the sea became calm.

There wasn't a storm out here this evening, Tessa reflected, but there was a hurricane raging inside both herself and Meg. She bent her head for a moment and closed her eyes, sending up another prayer for help; then she went on rowing, glancing back over her shoulder at intervals towards the island.

It was at that moment that the current caught them; it swept them along at a rate of knots and Tessa's heart started to pound as she turned and looked back over her shoulder. Suddenly, miraculously, they were in calm water again and quite close to the island which loomed large and eerie in the darkness. Two minutes later, *Seagull* bumped against a rock and the waves slapped coldly at her sides. Tessa shipped her oars and stood up stiffly. There was a convenient tree-stump nearby and she twisted the rope securely around it.

'What are we going to do?' Meg breathed.

'Get out, I suppose,' Tessa said wearily, almost past thinking. If Nick wasn't here . . . but her mind shied away from the thought.

Meg shrugged hopelessly and they stepped out on to a small patch of cold wet sand and looked around. A little path snaked its way through the undergrowth and Tessa walked towards it. Meg broke the silence, voicing both their thoughts. 'Wh-what's the good, Tessa?' she said, and sank hopelessly to the ground, burying her head in her hands.

Tessa went on without answering; Meg jumped to her feet again and stumbled after her. 'Don't leave me!' she pleaded.

They hadn't gone more than a short distance when something large and black loomed up before them in the darkness. A glimmer of starlight shone through an upright rectangular space and Tessa realised at once what it was – the entrance to an old tumble-down building. It was the derelict cottage!

At that moment Meg caught her breath as Tessa, not looking where she was going, tripped over something and went flying through the air. 'Ouch!' she shouted as she came to rest flat on her face in a clump of bracken and stinging-nettles. Meg screamed, her nerves in shreds, but Tessa was on her feet again in a trice. Next moment a whoop of joy rang out on the night air, awakening the gulls to a cacophony of sound and even penetrating her cousin's dulled senses.

'It's *him*, Meg!' Tessa yelled ecstatically. 'I tripped over his foot!'

Meg came to life, hurling herself at the prone figure of her brother stretched out on the ground. 'Nick!' she shouted hysterically; whilst Tessa, her knees buckling under her, dropped to the ground beside her, waves of relief flooding over her. She sat back on her heels after a moment and looked at Meg, a puzzled frown on her face. 'How on earth did he get here?' she murmured.

Meg shook her head in bewilderment; they had found him and that was all that mattered for the moment.

Nick lay a few yards from the door of the cottage; his eyes were closed, his face ghastly pale. Sodden, wearing only a pair of shorts, he was shivering as though he had the ague. His legs, arms and hands were covered in deep gashes and scratches, some of which were bleeding quite freely. A clump of jagged rocks stuck up through the scrub immediately behind him.

A new terror seized Meg. 'Is . . . is he dead?' she breathed.

Tessa put her ear to his chest and listened. 'It's beating – just about! . . . He's probably unconscious though.' As if to prove her wrong however, Nick's eyelids fluttered open at that moment, flickered and closed again. Tessa felt for his pulse, and as she did so a pair of wildly-staring eyes attempted to focus themselves on the faces bent over him. Nick struggled to sit up, gingerly touching the back of his head.

'Suffering from shock, I expect,' Tessa said. 'Give him the anorak, Meg.'

Meg leapt to obey, placing it tenderly around his shoulders.

'Ouch! My head!' he muttered, and fell back with a

groan. He lay still for a moment, then rolled his eyes fearfully towards the doorway of the cottage. He opened his mouth to speak again but appeared to think better of it.

'It's me Nick!' Meg bent over him soothingly. 'H-how do you feel?'

'Rotten!' he grunted.

'I'm not surprised!' Tessa said unfeelingly. She looked at his wounds, then nodded towards the rocks behind him. 'He must have tripped over those,' she told Meg.

Their patient was reviving now. He overheard and a shudder passed through him. He shook his head in feeble disagreement.

'Do you feel like sitting up now?' Tessa asked.

'Yep, let's go!' he muttered hoarsely. He tried to raise himself but fell back with a groan.

'You'd better lie still a bit longer,' she told him briskly; for now that her cousin was showing signs of improvement, any sympathy she had first felt was fast ebbing away. What an idiot the boy was, to be sure; it was time to ask the sixty-four thousand dollar question!

'Do you mind telling us how you got here?'

'Yes, how *did* you get here?' Meg echoed wonderingly.

There was no answer. The girls looked at each other.

'Someone picked him up in a boat, perhaps!' Meg suggested in an undertone.

'Must have done! He never swam!'

Nick sighed wearily. 'I . . . I got carried by the current,' he said at last.

Tessa gaped. 'By the current!' she gasped.

'I swam some of the way, then I got carried along by the current,' he repeated in a tired voice. 'Thought I was going to miss the island at first . . . Managed to grab hold of a rock as I went past . . . and come ashore!'

There was a short silence whilst the girls digested this astonishing piece of information.

'Just like that!' murmured Tessa weakly. 'And you nearly cut yourself to death in the process by the look of it,' she added.

'You might have been swept out to sea!' Meg breathed.

He struggled to sit up again. 'Well, I didn't, so that's that!' he said with a touch of his old bravado.

Tessa shook her head and sighed. 'Come on,' she said. 'We've got to get him home; he'll need antiseptic on those wounds. Give me a hand, Meg, we'll try and get him sitting up first.'

They eased him into a more upright position, propping him against one of the flatter rocks. There was a nasty gash on the back of his head which was bleeding quite a bit.

'Something clouted me!' Nick muttered through clenched teeth.

'With rocks all over the place, what can you expect?' Tess said shortly. 'It was either these rocks here, or you did it when you landed.'

'That wasn't rocks – not my head!' Nick averred, regardless of grammar.

'What was it, then?'

'I told you, something clouted me,' he repeated doggedly. 'A *thing*!' he added through clenched teeth.

'Is he wandering?' Meg asked fearfully.

'A bit concussed, I'd say. I've got a handkerchief in my pocket and there's another in the anorak. We'll knot them together.' It didn't take long to form a bandage. Tessa bound it tightly in place, then took her club badge from her jacket and secured the ends.

'That should stop it!' she said. 'We're getting you up, Nick. Right?'

He nodded glumly and the girls put a hand under each armpit and hauled him to his feet. He took a few tottery steps.

'You'll do!' Tessa said grimly. 'We'll get him straight back to the boat,' she told Meg.

They set off slowly, Nick with an arm around each of their shoulders. 'You all right, Nick?' his sister murmured compassionately, after a few yards.

'Head's throbbing like mad!' he complained scowlingly.

'Better have a rest then,' Tessa said abruptly.

36

Nick himself over-ruled this however. 'Keep going!' he mumbled, glancing back towards the cottage.

They made slow progress but reached the boat at last. The dinghy rocked precariously as Meg helped her brother aboard. Now that Nick was safely restored to them, problems of a different kind began to loom large on the horizon. She didn't dare contemplate what lay in store for them when they got back to the guest-house.

Tessa, too, was silent as she stepped into the dinghy. There was the return journey to face, and she was feeling whacked. She untied the mooring rope and shoved off with the oar, the boat glided smoothly forward over the inky, shining sea and they were away. With her cousins huddled together in the stern, she pulled hard for the shore and breathed a silent 'thank you' to God that her prayers had been answered.

'It's been awful!' she heard Meg whisper to her brother when they were a few hundred yards out from the island. 'Aunt and Uncle will be furious!'

'*Not half they won't*!' Tessa thought grimly. She looked at Nick, slouched beside his sister, elbows on knees, chin resting in his hands; he appeared oddly indifferent.

'Well, you shouldn't have raised a hue and cry,' he muttered ungraciously.

'What else could I do?' Meg complained, and began to weep again. 'I couldn't leave you to drown!'

He didn't answer, and Tessa glanced at her watch.

'It's nearly midnight!' she said.

At that moment Nick raised his head and stared with a glazed expression in his eyes towards the island fast receding into the night. His next words shook both girls rigid.

'That place really *is* haunted!' he muttered through taut, white lips.

Chapter 5

The Rescue

'Haunted!' Meg gasped, turning ghastly pale again.

'Haunted!' Tessa echoed, an expression of sheer disbelief leaping into her eyes . . . Then her mind went back to the first evening of the holidays. They had all been standing on the cliff-top above Sandy Bay and she remembered the nickname her cousin had given the island.

This was no time for joking, though, she told herself, and cast him a look that was a mixture of pity and contempt; he had turned pale and shivery again and the makeshift bandage had slipped down over his eyes, giving him a rakish appearance. Had the blow from the rock affected his brain? she wondered uneasily. But no, of course it hadn't, she told herself next minute; he *was* probably a bit concussed and needed to see a doctor.

'I tell you it's *haunted*!' Nick repeated, still staring towards the island fast merging into the shadows. He took a deep breath and went on in a low, hoarse voice, 'I felt pretty shattered after I got washed up there. I couldn't move for a bit! Then I got so shrammed lying on the wet sand that I decided to try and . . .'

'What about *me*!' Meg burst in indignantly, for now that Nick was safe it was herself she was beginning to feel sorry for. 'You never even though how I'd be feeling, did you, when you left me on the beach? . . . I told you not to go . . . I – it's been awful!' and she started to sob again.

Nick shrugged and sighed. 'Couldn't do much about it, could I, stuck over there?' He looked at Meg's distraught face and felt a bit guilty. 'Sorry, Sis, I really am. I thought it would be easy.'

'*Easy*!' Tessa muttered, pulling hard on the oars. She shook her head incredulously.

'Oh, forget it!' Meg sighed. Then, remembering what he had said, and overcome with curiosity, she asked, 'What do you mean about the island being haunted?'

Nick drew a long breath. 'I didn't hit my head on those rocks,' he said, looking steadily at Tessa.

'What happened, then?' Meg asked sharply.

There was a short silence; the girls looked at him.

'It was the ghost!' he said at last.

Tessa stared blankly. The only sound to be heard was the creaking of the oars and the swish of water off the blades. The blow had definitely affected him, she decided. 'You've got ghosts on the brain,' she retorted.

Nick ignored her; the shocked look was beginning to recede again; he seemed more like himself. 'As I say, I got frozen lying there,' he went on, 'so I decided to look for somewhere more sheltered. I found the path and came to the cottage.'

'And what happened?' Meg breathed.

'It was a bit creepy but I don't believe in spooks and all that kind of thing. At least I didn't!' he added grimly, pursing his lips.

Tessa rowed on wearily. 'Well . . . what happened then?' she echoed absently, more concerned with getting them all safely ashore than with listening to her cousin's fanciful ramblings.

'I went up to the door of the cottage and looked inside. And there was this *thing*!' He looked at Tessa again. 'It was white from head to foot. I couldn't have imagined it. I saw it standing there with my own eyes as clearly as I see you! . . . Then I started to run and . . .'

'And what?' Tessa encouraged, faintly intrigued. As for Meg, her eyes grew rounder and rounder as she waited for her brother to continue.

'And then,' Nick said quietly, 'it must have given me a terrific clout!' He put up a cautious hand and touched the back of his head as though to give his words credence. 'I slipped and fell and I don't remember anything more until you two came along.'

They had reached the shore at last and as the bottom of the boat bumped onto the sand, Tessa shipped her oars and stood up. Utterly exhausted by now and feeling slightly hysterical, she wasn't sure whether to be angry or to collapse into giggles. It was no laughing matter, though; her parents would be absolutely furious about the whole thing.

'It was the starlight shining through the windows,' she said matter-of-factly. 'I told you what happened – you slipped and knocked your head on a rock.' She stepped out on to the beach and held the boat steady, and Meg got out, too, giving her brother a helping hand and an anxious, frightened look at the same time.

'Ghosts don't usually go around clouting people over the head,' Tessa continued as no one spoke. 'At least I don't think they do,' she added sarcastically, 'but then I've never met one!' She hitched the mooring rope over her shoulder and prepared to haul the rowing-boat back up the beach. As she did so, she cast another pitying glance in Nick's direction.

He sighed resignedly and shook his head. Further argument was going to be useless: that much was obvious.

'I'll just help Tessa with the boat,' Meg said, giving her brother another worried look. 'Don't hurry, Nick! We'll wait for you at the top.'

So while the two girls pulled *Seagull* back up the beach, Nick limped slowly after them, taking his time about it. For by now he was beginning to feel stiff in every joint.

'We'll leave it just here out of reach of the tide,' Tessa told Meg. 'It'll have to stay there till tomorrow.' Then they climbed the cliff path, a weary little procession, Nick leaning heavily on his sister for support.

Tessa was first up. No sooner had she reached the top than she stopped dead, staring intently across the fields over to their right, her attention riveted. Following her

40

gaze and straining their eyes into the darkness, Nick and Meg saw a small knot of people hurrying towards them. They exchanged apprehensive glances; though this time it was something more substantial than ghosts that was worrying them!

'They're out searching for us,' Tessa murmured. 'I knew they would be!'

'Don't tell on us, Tess!' Meg pleaded.

'I shan't say anything,' Tessa shrugged.

Nick looked at his sister. 'We'll have to make up something,' he muttered. 'We'll just have to say we got lost!'

Meg bit her lip and looked at Tessa. Nick looked at her, too, but she shook her head. 'They'll see through it,' she told them. 'Anyway, we can't tell lies.'

'Spoil-sport!' Nick burst out.

'Well, at least I rescued you,' Tessa pointed out, not unreasonably.

'It's no good,' Meg said flatly. 'Tessa's right. They'll never believe us.'

The group was almost on them now, flashing torches as they came across the field adjacent to the cliff path. In the dim light Tessa made out the figure of the local policeman walking ahead with her father. Behind was her mother with a twin on either side and Badger bringing up the rear. Panic-stricken now, Nick and Meg moved closer to one another for mutual support. Police Sergeant Perkins detached himself from the group and came striding towards them.

'Now then, what's all this about?' he asked, subjecting each of them to a searching scrutiny. 'I understand from your parents you've all been missing for the last three hours.'

As no one spoke, Bob MacLaren stepped forward and looked enquiringly at his daughter. 'Joan Trembath came round about ten-thirty to say that Nick and Meg had not come to bed. We then discovered you were missing too, Tessa. Martha said you were in at ten looking at the kittens. Now what have you all been up to?' he asked sternly.

There was another lengthy pause. Tessa had no intention of telling tales and the other two seemed completely tongue-tied.

'What's the matter with Nick's head?' his aunt asked suddenly, noticing the bandage.

Tessa took a deep breath and studied her sandals. 'I think Nick should get straight back home,' she said at last. 'He – er – had a bit of an accident; hit the back of his head and it's been bleeding quite a lot . . .'

Nick snorted. 'I *didn't* hit it!' he scowled. 'It was that bloomin . . .'

Peter interrupted, unable to contain himself. 'Where've you all been, then?' he said with disconcerting directness.

'You don't half look pale, Nick,' Paula added. 'Just as though you'd seen a ghost!'

This was too much for Tessa; she went off into helpless giggles. She pulled herself together with an effort as Nick glared at her.

'It's nothing to laugh at,' he mumbled aggrievedly.

'Are you sure you're all right, Nick?' his aunt asked, eyeing her nephew anxiously and misunderstanding the reason for his annoyance. 'How did you . . . ?'

'Oh, it's OK now,' Nick interrupted in a surly voice. He looked at the policeman and then at his uncle, and wondered what his chances were of making a dash for it. Sergeant Perkins exchanged glances with Bob and Jane MacLaren.

'I'll be getting back now . . . Leave the rest to you, sir,' he added in an aside.

'Right! Thanks for your help, Sergeant . . . Now come on, children! Let's get going. It's gone midnight and it's high time you were all in bed.'

'Certainly is – keeping respectable folk out at this hour o' the night,' Sergeant Perkins grumbled with a bit of a grin. 'OK, sir! All in a day's . . . er, night's work! . . . Goodnight Mrs MacLaren! Night all!'

42

A chorus of 'Goodnights' rang out on the night air as the policeman strode off in the direction of the town. There was a short pause before Bob MacLaren said briskly, 'Well, we'll leave explanations until tomorrow morning – er, till the morning,' he amended, 'unless anyone feels inclined to enlighten me before!' He glanced at his watch. 'Now come along, all of you, let's get going!'

They set off along the cliff-top towards the village in an uneasy silence broken only by the chatter of the younger children.

'I'm tired!' piped up Paula, dragging her feet as she clutched her mother's hand.

'We've scoured the countryside for miles!' her brother added excitedly, 'Glad you let us come, Mum!'

'I wouldn't have if you hadn't made such a fuss about being left behind,' his mother reminded him.

'Not far to go now,' Bob MacLaren encouraged as they turned off the cliff path on to the hill. He had positioned immediately behind Nick and Meg all the way back, so as to keep an eye on them. Now, as he looked at the two miscreants marching silently ahead of him, his eyes slid sideways to meet Tessa's.

She encountered his puzzled gaze and pulled a wry face. She wasn't going to inform on them, no way! She would go straight to bed and leave it to her cousins to do the explaining.

They were at the top of the hill now.

'Sorry about all the bother,' Tessa told her parents in an aside as they stopped outside the little white gate of Martha's cottage. 'Don't be too hard on them,' she breathed into her father's ear. Then, glancing at Nick and Meg hovering uncertainly on the pavement, she murmured, 'See you in the morning!' and disappeared up the path into the cottage.

It wasn't until she had reached the seclusion of the little bedroom under the eaves that she realised she was feeling absolutely dead-beat. As she sank onto the bed Nick's voice, slightly desperate-sounding, came wafting up to her through the lattice window.

'I . . . I suppose it's all my fault for swimming out there,' he was saying in an agitated voice. 'Tessa doesn't believe me but . . . but . . . !'

'But what?' his uncle asked severely.

'That island really *is* haunted!'

'*Haunted*! What on earth do you mean, Nick?' Her mother sounded absolutely stunned.

Tessa held her breath, and waited. There was a short pause before her father spoke and when he did his voice seemed ominously calm.

'*You swam out?*' he repeated slowly and with heavy emphasis. '*To the Island?*'

Chapter 6

The Day After

Meg woke late next morning to the realisation that something disastrous had happened; it didn't take her long to remember what! She and Nick had had the telling-off of a lifetime from Uncle Bob in the early hours of the morning. Her brother had soon discovered that his uncle wasn't in the least impressed by his story of a ghost.

He was hopping mad about their escapade, though! They had had absolutely no right, he pointed out, to be down on the beach when they were supposed to be in bed; Nick had been specifically warned of the dangers of swimming out to sea and he deserved to be confined to the house for the whole of the following day. As it was Sunday, however, he would be expected to go to church in the morning (something he and Meg had managed to get out of the previous Sunday). He would let him know about the picnic in the afternoon when he had given the question further thought.

Nick was by that time past caring whether he went or not; the dressing down from his uncle had left him wilting. He would have been given a severe thrashing if he'd been his own son, Uncle Bob had informed him. Later, when his aunt had bathed and bandaged his wounds, he fell into bed feeling sick and dizzy.

As for Meg, she got off a little more lightly. She was weak and easily led, her uncle told her severely; she should have the courage to stand out against her brother's wild schemes! He hoped she would go along to church tomorrow though, with the others and as a special concession she could go to the picnic in the afternoon, too, provided there was no more trouble.

Thinking things over before she fell into a disturbed sleep, Meg was surprised to discover that going to church seemed to be the least of her worries. The trip to the island was another matter, however; she felt she never wanted to see the place again as long as she lived.

Breakfast was at eight-thirty on Sundays and it was gone nine when Nick woke. Feeling slightly less shattered after his few hours sleep, but still pretty washed out, he quickly pulled on his clothes and went out on to the landing. Meg was waiting for him, looking chastened and apprehensive.

'They can't eat us!' Nick said philosophically.

'I dunno so much, you've really been and gone and done it this time, haven't you?' She looked at his bandaged head and relented. 'You feeling better?' she asked anxiously.

'Not bad!' he shrugged.

They descended the stairs in silence; neither was sorry to find that their uncle and aunt had breakfasted early and gone. Only Tessa, Peter and Paula were seated round the table in the dining-room.

'Hello there!' Tessa said and busied herself with her boiled egg, avoiding their eyes. An awkward pause followed as they took their seats. 'Pour yourselves tea,' she told them, 'and help yourselves to cornflakes or whatever you want.'

They muttered a greeting and did as they were told. The twins watched surreptitiously; only Tessa made any attempt at conversation but it was heavy going. As for Meg, every mouthful she took seemed to stick in her throat.

'There's a parade service at church this morning,' Tessa said presently.

'How long will church last?' Meg asked nervously; Nick hadn't said whether he was going or not, but she intended to be there anyway. For once she had made up her own mind about something independently of her brother.

'About an hour,' Tessa told her. 'I'm reading a lesson!'

There was another silence. Peter looked at Nick. 'You going to the island?' he asked, curiosity getting the better of him. It was a taboo subject this morning and Tessa frowned. Nick frowned too and said nothing; he'd no intention of discussing the matter with this cheeky youngster! He didn't care whether he went or not anyway, or so he told himself; he'd had enough of the island for the time being!

Looking out of the window a moment later, however, he changed his mind. The sun was climbing higher and higher in the sky; it looked like being a scorcher. It would be too bad if he were to be cooped up indoors all afternoon. Would his uncle relent and let him go, he wondered.

Tessa got up at last, 'Clear the table, twins, won't you! I'm taking Badger for a walk. See you later!'

When she had gone, a mischievous gleam leapt into Peter's eyes. He looked at Nick. 'Can't wait for the picnic!' he said, throwing caution to the winds.

Nick frowned again and said nothing.

'What's over there?' Paula asked.

'Nothing much!' Meg shrugged.

'Ghosts!' Peter muttered under his breath, and Paula nearly choked into her tea. Nick looked daggers at both of them.

'Tessa says there are no such things,' Paula stuttered, blowing her nose.

'Nick says there are!' Peter said with a wink.

This was too much for Nick; something snapped inside him. He turned pale and glowered. 'Shut up, you kids! You both need a jolly good hiding!'

'Well, that's what you told Mum and Dad last night,' Peter said defensively. 'We couldn't help hearing.'

'You shouldn't have been listening, jug-ears!' Nick retorted. 'Mind your own business, right?' He gulped down his last piece of toast and got to his feet. 'Come on, Meg, let's go!'

They went out into the garden. Neither of them spoke

for a moment. Meg looked at her brother's face. It was crimson.

'That thing you saw last night,' she said slowly. 'Was it really a ghost?'

'I dunno,' he muttered. 'It certainly looked like one.'

They were silent again.

'What are we going to do about it?' Meg asked at last. 'We'll never hear the end of it!'

Nick shrugged and shook his head. 'I dunno . . . yet.'

They hung around until Tessa returned from her walk with Badger. 'You going to church?' Nick muttered to his sister.

'Yes, are you?'

He looked surprised. 'S'pose so,' he said grudgingly. 'Haven't much choice!'

The twins joined them and the five children set off. The little old Saxon building was full when they got there. Tessa led the way up to the front, though Nick with his bandaged head would rather have slipped into a back pew; he wondered what he would say if he were asked about it. He looked around and his eyes widened with surprise. Chris from the camp-site was sitting a few rows back on his own. Life suddenly took on a more interesting note again!

The service started off with a good rousing hymn. Later, Tessa went up to the front to read the lesson. It was about the parable of the Sower and she read it slowly and distinctly so that Meg found herself listening in spite of herself. She glanced sideways at her brother; he was jingling the money in his pocket and seemed miles away.

He came alive again at the end of it all, however, and stared curiously at Chris as they passed his pew on the way out. They stepped out of the porch into the sunshine.

'It wasn't bad, was it!' Meg ventured.

Nick shrugged and glanced back over his shoulder, still thinking about Chris. He hadn't expected to see him in church, somehow . . .

They walked down the path between the tombstones. Tessa had gone on ahead and was standing by the lychgate talking to some of her friends. Was she telling them about last night? Meg wondered uneasily. As for Nick, he started thinking about his bandaged head again; questions were bound to be asked, he told himself. He'd just have to concoct something.

Tessa beckoned them over at that moment. She was looking quite friendly, Meg noticed – almost as though nothing much had happened. 'Perhaps she's decided to exercise Christian charity and forgive and forget,' Nick thought cynically as they came level with the group.

'We're just arranging about this afternoon,' Tessa explained. 'Are you both coming?'

Meg looked at Nick; he muttered under his breath that it wasn't up to him.

'Dad told me just now that you're both coming – if you want to, that is,' Tessa told him.

'Oh, right!' Nick said, his spirits rising. Meg said nothing.

'That's good, it should be fun!' Tessa enthused.

'I – I don't think I shall go,' Meg whispered to her brother; but he wasn't listening and she saw that he was staring back towards the church. At that moment Bob MacLaren came along; he had been singing in the choir.

'You gave Nick the message about this afternoon?' he asked Tessa in an undertone.

'Yes, and they're both coming, I think . . .'

Perhaps she would go after all, Meg thought; it would be better than staying at home on her own all afternoon.

They all walked home together. Nick was still thinking about the lone camper. There had been no sign of him outside the church; he must have slipped away by a side door, he supposed . . . Next minute he pricked up his ears.

'Chris from the camp-site was in church, Dad,' Tessa remarked.

'That's good!' said her father.

'Do you know him?' Nick butted in quickly, before her father could reply.

His cousin looked surprised. 'He played tennis with us last Friday. He's a good tennis-player,' she said.

* * *

They set off for the harbour soon after lunch, carrying their picnic teas in string bags. At the last moment Meg had reluctantly decided to go.

There was quite a crowd gathered on the quay when they got there, and *Golden Spray* was moored alongside. Bob MacLaren had gone on ahead and was already aboard the launch. Nick looked around for Chris again but there was no sign of him, neither did he turn up by the time they were ready to sail.

'All aboard!' Bob MacLaren shouted through cupped hands. The children crowded down the stone steps and on to the boat, chattering excitedly.

'I wonder if we'll see any ghosts over there,' Peter whispered to Tessa, and Paula started giggling.

'Shut up!' Tessa warned. 'It's not funny, you know! Dad says we're not to joke about it, Nick could have been drowned; it was very stupid of him . . . We're not to talk about it to the others, either,' she warned. Though even as she spoke she felt doubtful that the twins would be able to keep the story to themselves.

Everyone with the exception of Meg enjoyed the trip over; even Nick was beginning to savour life again. Peter and Paula hung over the side of the boat relishing every minute. The water was so clear they could see all the plants growing on the sandy ocean bed.

Meg stared towards the island as they approached. In the light of day it appeared a whole lot less grim and terrifying than it had done the night before; so much so that she wondered whether it had all been a ghastly nightmare – except when she looked at Nick's head. Then it was real enough!

50

'There's the cottage,' he murmured

They chugged closer and Meg glanced furtively at her brother. He was standing a little apart from them, staring intently towards the granite outcrop. There was a pensive expression in his eyes and it wasn't difficult to guess what he was thinking about. What was it that Nick had seen over there? she asked herself for the umpteenth time.

Tessa broke into her thoughts. 'There's a landing stage around the other side, Dad says.' She lowered her voice. 'We won't be getting off where we did last night.'

Meg shivered as everything came flooding back. 'I . . . I wish I hadn't come, Tess,' she sighed.

Tessa shrugged. 'Well, you're here now so you may as well make the best of it,' she said briskly. Then, thinking that sounded a bit blunt, she added, 'If it's the ghost you're worrying about, then don't! It was all imagination!'

'I suppose so,' Meg sighed, only half convinced.

'He wasn't really in a position to tell, was he?' her cousin reasoned. 'I mean, he was practically unconscious when we saw him.'

'I suppose so,' Meg said again.

'Forget it!' Tessa told her. 'It's all over and done with!'

Golden Spray was sailing close to the west side of the island now, coming round to the southern aspect which faced the open sea. Tessa looked eagerly towards it; it seemed transformed by daylight. A small broken-down jetty came into view.

'That's where we land,' she said, and Nick came suddenly to life.

'There's the cottage,' he murmured, breaking a long silence.

'It – looks different,' Meg mused.

'That's because we're seeing it from the other side,' Tessa explained. She glanced curiously at Nick; he appeared to be on another planet as he gazed fixedly towards the island.

Chapter 7

On the Island Again

Golden Spray drew alongside the little broken-down jetty and Bob MacLaren threw the anchor overboard. It fell into the sea with a splash and everyone crowded to the side of the boat, eager to get off.

Steve stood ready with a helping hand. 'One at a time now, we don't want anyone overboard! It's three o'clock now; you've got an hour to explore. Be back here for tea at four prompt.'

'You can leave your picnic teas with us; we'll look after them for you and we promise not to eat them!' Bob MacLaren added.

Laughter greeted this remark as the children scrambled down on to the landing-stage. They set off, some following the beach round to the left, others making for the rocks on the opposite side.

Tessa, still on the boat with Melanie, glanced curiously at Nick and Meg waiting to disembark. Nick caught her eye and looked the other way. 'If they want to go off on their own, that's OK by us!' Tessa said. 'They can't come to much harm, anyway – at least, I hope not!'

Melanie looked mystified. 'What's Nick done to his head?' she asked.

'If you promise not to tell . . .'

'You can trust me!'

'All right! Wait till we get off.'

Tessa looked at her cousins again as they stepped off the launch and her gaze followed them as they set off across the beach. Neither appeared to be talking; Nick was staring fixedly towards the centre of the island, his sister looked uneasy. She was surprised to see them making for the path that led to the ruined cottage.

'Meg looks fed up!' Melanie remarked.

'With good reason!' Tessa said cryptically.

The two girls got off the boat. David was waiting for them with Sheba and the three friends strolled off together in the direction of the rocks. Tessa had to confide in someone and she knew she could trust these two. She quickly related the events of the previous evening.

'Phew!' Melanie said when she had finished. 'Some adventure!'

'Nick should have learned his lesson after that lot anyway,' David said thoughtfully. 'Some people have to find out the hard way,' he added, with a teasing look in Tessa's direction.

She pulled a face; she knew he was thinking of the time he had come to her rescue when she got cut off by the tide. 'I mustn't be too hard on him, I suppose,' she said soberly. 'It's a bit like the kettle calling the pot black!'

*   *   *

Meanwhile Nick and Meg had reached the path that led to the centre of the island. Nick's thirst for adventure had suffered only a temporary setback; he was a glutton for punishment, as his sister had told him!

Scrub-land interspersed with flaming yellow gorse and ling stretched away on either side of them; Meg was in no mood to appreciate the beauties of nature, though. Remembering Uncle Bob's words, she had done her best to talk Nick out of returning to the cottage, but her objections had been over-ruled. Her brother was adamant; he was going and she was going with him willy-nilly . . . for if the truth were told he didn't fancy making the visit on his own!

Both children stopped dead in their tracks when they saw the cottage. Tall trees obscured the sunlight and a tangle of bushes surrounded the crumbling ruin. There was something vaguely sinister about the place and Nick had the strange impression someone was watching them . . .

He went on and his sister followed reluctantly. They passed a small side door: a rusty key was still in the lock. Meg caught her breath as they came round to the front. Part of the roof had fallen in but the granite walls stood four-square; daylight filtered through into the dim recesses below. The front door hung drunkenly on its hinges and a lot of rubble and masonry lay on the ground.

Nick stared at it without speaking; Meg shivered. Branches forced their way through the stonework; they sprouted out through the roof, the chimney and the unglazed windows like twisted, malformed limbs. Even by daylight the cottage looked eerie.

A little way from the entrance, flattened gorse and heather marked the spot where Nick had been lying when Tessa and Meg had found him. There was no one about, nobody else had penetrated as far as the cottage. Nick's spine prickled a bit and Meg turned pale.

'Come on, Nick, let's go!' she pleaded, but he only shrugged.

'If you don't want to come, wait here!' he told her as he stepped over the threshold into the cottage.

Meg hesitated for only a moment; the events of last night had shaken her to the core and as she looked at her brother something rose up within her and she rebelled. There was no point in meddling in things one didn't understand, she told herself; no good could come of it! She delivered her ultimatum.

'You can do as you like,' she said. 'I'm going back!' and she turned on her heel and walked rapidly away along the path. Nick frowned to himself; she had never deserted him like that before and he looked around uneasily. The place was creepy enough and he had half a mind to follow her.

Curiosity overcoming all other considerations, however, he decided against it and looked around. The cottage had consisted of one large room downstairs, plus a smaller one, possibly a kitchen, on the right-hand side. There were the remains of a stone staircase against the far wall which had once given access to an upstairs room. The floorboards were badly rotted; the place had gone to wrack and ruin.

He had taken this much in when his attention was attracted by something on the ground in the far left-hand corner of the room. He walked across the uneven floor to inspect it more closely; it was a small pile of ashes and as he stood looking down at it an idea leapt into his head. It was at that precise moment that he had the uncanny feeling again that he was not alone.

He swung round, his heart thudding. A shudder ran down his spine, then suddenly he relaxed! . . . It was only the dark-haired girl Melanie, Tessa's friend, and he breathed again. Sheba stood beside her, tongue lolling out, tail swinging slowly from side to side. He could have sworn the dog was grinning at him . . .

Melanie looked apologetic. 'Hello!' she said. 'Sorry if I startled you!'

Nick grunted, feeling a fool. She must have noticed how scared he'd looked! . . . He remembered his bandaged head and wondered whether she'd got to hear about last night . . .

Her expression gave nothing away, however; she looked friendly enough. After the initial shock, he decided he was quite pleased to see her – now that Meg had chickened out and deserted him.

'Sheba ran off after a rabbit or something. We went different ways looking for him,' Melanie explained. 'Goodness knows where Dave and Tessa have got to, though!'

'Just having a poke round,' Nick said casually. 'Funny old place this!'

'It is, isn't it?' She gave him a swift appraising glance,

A venomous pair of eyes treated her to a hostile, unblinking stare

then stepped beneath the sloping, worm-eaten lintel, glancing round at the rough walls and up at the roof festooned with branches and leaves. Through one of the windows the sea, tranquil as a lake, stretched away to the distant shore and she stood looking at it for a moment. It was so quiet and peaceful that when next moment an ear-piercing shriek shattered the silence, echoing hollowly inside the dilapidated roof and reverberating around the crumbling walls, both children jumped a foot or two into the air.

Melanie was the first to recover. She went quickly outside and looked up at the roof. A venomous pair of eyes treated her to a hostile, unblinking stare and it didn't take her long to realise that they belonged to a greater black-backed gull perched on the chimney-pot. She went off into a paroxysm of laughter. 'He's telling us we're trespassing!' she gasped between her giggles.

Nick joined her outside and glared white-faced at the evil-looking creature. It had frightened him nearly silly. He must still be in a state of shock after last night, he told himself, otherwise he'd never have been terrified out of his wits by a mere gull. 'Should think it's nearly tea-time,' he muttered, feeling foolish again.

Melanie looked at her watch. 'Help, so it is, how the time's gone! Fascinating places, islands!' she went on conversationally.

'Not half!' he lied. Secretly he felt he never wanted to set foot on one again.

They were about to leave the cottage when Melanie happened to glance behind the door. She bent down suddenly. There was a piece of paper sticking out from under a small rock; it looked like part of a page torn from an exercise book. She pulled it out and smoothed it flat. There was some writing on it but it didn't make much sense to her, nor to Nick peering over her shoulder.

'One of the others must have been here,' she said. 'Looks as though it's just been dropped.'

Nick took the bit of paper from her and a strange expression crept into his eyes. He was sure no one else had been near the ruined cottage!

'Maybe!' he said off-handedly and put it carefully into the pocket of his jeans. Chris hadn't turned up this afternoon, he thought inconsequentially. They walked back to join the others.

*　　*　　*

Most of the children had returned when Nick and Melanie got back to the landing beach. There was a babel of conversation going on; nearly all had found time to walk round the island and explore the beaches. Not one, Nick suspected, in spite of what Melanie had said, had visited the ruined cottage apart from himself, her and Meg. As far as he was concerned the incident had left him with plenty to think about.

They spread out over the beach with their picnic teas, facing across the open sea to the distant horizon. Even the reef appeared less forbidding than when the children had viewed it from the cliff-top on the first evening of the holidays. Foam-flecked, the habitat of numerous seals and scores of sea-birds, it looked harmless enough in broad daylight. The 'whirligigs' the twins had talked about were invisible from that distance.

Mostly the ocean lay still as a lily pond in the heat-haze, though to the left of the beach the current raced, eddied, and boiled between the granite rocks. Meg, sitting between Tessa and David, looked at the patch of turbulent water and shivered, reliving the horrors of the night. Her brother, however, safely away from the cottage, felt his courage return. Sitting next to Melanie in a companionable silence, he stuffed himself with Cornish pasty and lobster sandwiches, and his spirits rose as he surveyed the majestic scene. Already he felt himself coming under the spell of this wild and rugged coastline.

His head had stopped throbbing, too, by now and the

salt water had begun a healing process on his wounds. The nightmare experience of being carried out to sea by the current like a piece of flotsam wouldn't go away so easily, however. He recalled his utter relief as the hulk of the island had loomed into view, sinister but welcome. He wouldn't land up in America after all, he remembered thinking!

Being literally tossed up on to the rock-bound shore with little in the way of effort on his part, had been a painful experience by any reckoning; though even this paled into insignificance compared with what had happened later. After lying exhausted on the beach for a good twenty minutes, shocked and shivering from the Arctic state of the night sea and the stiffish breeze blowing, he had got up and limped slowly and painfully along the prickly path between the gorse and heather in search of a more sheltered spot in which to bed down for the night. It was then that he had come upon the cottage, and what had occurred after that lingered on in his mind as more real than anything that had gone before.

His uncle could pour scorn on his story, his aunt could sigh and shake her head. As for Tessa and the twins, they could jeer to their hearts' content. He hadn't imagined anything, and he was sticking to his story! How to prove it, though, was another matter . . .

He stopped day-dreaming and came back to the present. Conversation buzzed around him; the gulls mewed plaintively, making greedy sorties every time a tit-bit came their way. He fingered the piece of paper in his pocket; he'd have a closer look at it when he got back . . . Would the story of the night leak out? he wondered; did Melanie know what had happened? If so, she had given no sign . . . He stared at the twins, giggling and whispering in the front row. At that moment they turned and saw him; broad grins spread over their freckled faces! Let them laugh, he told himself . . .

Over to the left Tessa was carrying on an animated conversation with David. Meg sat silently. The two dogs basked in the sunshine. He glanced sideways at Melanie; he was glad of her company for Meg had looked his way only once since they got back. Admittedly he had given his sister an awful fright but she would come round in a day or two, he told himself.

He finished his last sandwich, swilled it down with lemonade, then looked at Gary Travers and his friends sitting on the outskirts of the group. Even they were behaving themselves for once – under the spell of the island, too, maybe! An unwelcome thought struck him: if Gary got to hear about his adventure he might as well be dead!

* * *

There was a short service before they left for home, and being Sunday it lasted a bit longer than usual. Some of the youngsters had been running races on the beach and Steve talked about the great Marathon that took place through the streets of London each year. Thousands of people trained for weeks and weeks to run in the twenty-four-mile race in aid of charity. You couldn't hope to complete the course unless you had undergone strenuous training.

You certainly couldn't run in the Marathon – or any race – wearing a sweater, football boots or with a rucksack on your back, he said. 'Course you couldn't, Nick thought to himself, letting the sand trickle through his fingers and only half listening. As if anybody thought you could!

'Put aside every weight,' Steve continued, quoting from St Paul in the Bible, 'and run the race that is set before you.' Weights were not necessarily bad things, just anything that got in the way of winning the race . . .

Like doing his own thing, Nick supposed, still sifting sand. Well, it certainly hadn't done him much good this time, he told himself. As his uncle and aunt kept telling him, he was lucky to be alive! . . . He frowned suddenly;

61

he still wasn't sure whether or not God existed – though here on the island with the sun and the sea and the fresh air, it was easier to believe that he did . . .

*　　*　　*

'All aboard!' shouted Bob MacLaren as everyone headed towards the boat. The tide was running out rapidly now, rushing over the smooth firm sand and gurgling around the limpet-covered rocks. It trickled into the anemone-filled rock pools where tiny crabs scuttled across the sand and small fishes darted between fronds of seaweed. As the children hurried over the narrowing strip of sand towards the launch, Nick glanced back in the direction of the cottage, and there was a far-away look in his eyes.

Everybody clambered aboard *Golden Spray*, the skipper weighed anchor and they were away. A crowd of screeching gulls hovered overhead as the island receded into the distance, and someone was talking about the tern's nest he had almost stepped on whilst walking on one of the beaches. They chugged back to the mainland in a flurry of spray.

'See you all down at Kennet Sands on Wednesday afternoon for beach games!' Steve told everyone as they climbed up the steps to the quay.

Chapter 8

At the Camp-site

It was raining the following Wednesday, a fine damping drizzle. A thick mist blotted out the cliffs and sea and everything looked sodden.

'No beach games today, I'm afraid!' Bob MacLaren said at breakfast. 'It's going to be like this for the next twenty-four hours, according to the forecast.'

'Bother!' said Tessa, staring thoughtfully out of the window. 'What'll we do instead?'

'How about a visit to the natural history museum?' her father suggested. 'Unless anyone can come up with anything better.'

'That's an idea! We'd have to let everyone know, though.'

'That would be no problem. I'll contact Steve to see what he thinks!' He went into the hall to phone and was back in a few minutes. 'He's quite agreeable. Suggests two-thirty outside the museum . . . I've got to get off down to the harbour now to cancel my fishing trips; I'll leave you to let the others know.'

Her uncle gone, Meg looked quickly at Tessa, avoiding her brother's eyes. 'You and I could do the cottages together – unless you'd rather do the camp-site.'

'I'll do the camp-site!' Nick interrupted.

'OK, then,' said Tessa.

'I'll come with you and Meg,' Peter decided, looking at his elder sister.

'So will I!' said Paula with a swift sideways glance at Nick.

Nick frowned; they couldn't have made it more obvious that his company wasn't wanted. Ever since Meg had deserted him at the cottage there had been a subtle change in his sister's attitude. He thought back over the years; he'd led her into all sorts of scrapes – none as bad as this one, admittedly – and she'd supported him no matter what, been his willing ally.

Now suddenly, in one fell swoop, everything had altered. He put it down to Tessa's influence – plus the talking-to she'd had from Uncle Bob, most likely! What he thought of his uncle and cousins was nobody's business.

Tessa, Meg and the twins finished their breakfast and disappeared. Left on his own, Nick went out into the lobby. He put on his anorak, pulled the hood well down over his face, and went outside. The weather fitted his mood to perfection: he felt in the depths of gloom and despondency. There was one thing about it though; he'd got a genuine excuse to visit the camp-site again. There was a distinct possibility he might see the owner of the brown tent today, he thought. Being a wet day he would probably be around . . .

He set off through the thick fog and driving rain, hands thrust deep in pockets. Black clouds hung low overhead, the rain sheeted down on him; out to sea a bell-buoy tolled its melancholy warning to shipping. The remembrance of Meg's disloyalty rankled more and more with every step he took; he kicked viciously at a stone.

Arriving at the camp-site he pushed open the gate and trudged over the soggy grass between the dripping tents. With but one thought in mind his eyes went automatically to that part of the field where the brown tent stood. There was no sign of its owner though; sodden and deserted, it flapped forlornly in the wind.

He sighed and went on. Most of the campers were taking shelter inside their tents; parents were doing their best to keep the children out of mischief. Most looked pleased when Nick delivered his message; it would take the youngsters off their hands for part at least of what looked

like being a trying day. The kids perked up, too, on
hearing about the trip to the museum; it would be better
than hanging around the camp-site with nothing to do . . .

Nick tramped to the far end of the field. The scouts were
out and about despite the weather, busy with their chores.
He recognised some who had been at the barbecue; most
seemed quite keen on the museum idea. Having extended
the invitation to anyone else who appeared interested, he
retraced his steps. As far as the other matter was
concerned, however, it looked as though he was doomed
to disappointment. Nothing, but nothing, seemed to be
working out for him; he was no nearer to solving the
mystery of the island!

Almost level with the brown tent now, he looked
towards it and looked again. A tall figure in a yellow
sou'wester and waterproof had appeared on the other side
of the hedge dividing the camp-site from the adjoining
field. Nick came to an abrupt halt as he recognized his
quarry through a narrow gap in the hedge. Chris had a
pair of binoculars slung around his neck, and even as Nick
watched, he stopped beneath the spreading branches of
a large chestnut tree, raised the glasses to his eyes and
stared intently upwards through the dripping foliage.

Now for it, Nick told himself! He stepped quickly
forward and without stopping to think shouted, 'Hi!' At
that precise moment a small bird with a black head and
white on its rump fluttered off a nearby branch of the tree
and took wing into the mist. There was an exasperated
look on Chris's face as he lowered the binoculars and spun
round. 'That was a stupid thing to do!' he scowled and
turned abruptly away.

Nick grimaced. It wasn't a terribly good beginning, but
he wasn't to be that easily put off. This was his big chance,
he told himself, and advanced again, this time more
cautiously.

'There's no beach games this afternoon,' he called out
in lowered tones. 'They're doing a visit to the natural
history museum instead!'

Chris swung round again. 'What time?' he asked unexpectedly, and Nick took courage.

'Two-thirty outside the museum.'

Chris looked down at the gound. 'Thanks!' he said shortly and turned away again. Nick's suspicions grew; the chap was trying to avoid him, that much was obvious. The question was, Why? He took a deep breath.

'You didn't make the island trip, then!' he said.

A guarded expression crept into Chris's eyes; 'Couldn't manage it!' he said shortly and strode off towards the brown tent.

With no excuse to linger, Nick squelched his way back to the gate. He was feeling more cheerful now though; Chris had definitely looked odd at the mention of the island. He left the camp-site and whistled his way back along the muddy, puddly lane until he reached the road.

He was passing the village shop a few minutes later when two figures emerged. They were draped in macs almost down to their ankles and sucking lollies; he practically collided with one of them – it was Gary Travers! Should he tell them about the museum trip? he asked himself. Gary nudged his friend at that moment, however, and muttered into his ear. It would be best to ignore them, Nick decided, but Gary had other ideas.

'Hi, there! Been swimming lately?' he shouted.

Nick scowled; there was no mistaking his meaning. Before he could think up a suitable reply Gary's friend asked innocently, 'Seen any more ghosts, then?'

Anger rose up in Nick; someone had been talking! As the two boys slouched rapidly away down the road, grinning and splashing in all the puddles they could find, he clenched his fists and started after them.

'I'll punch their noses for them!' he muttered, but changed his mind next moment. It'd be two to one and he'd be bound to get the worst of it . . . Someone would pay for this though, he told himself furiously as he hurried back to the guest-house!

Tessa and Meg were just going in through the side door

when he got there. He followed as they turned into the annexe chattering like old friends. They went into the games-room and he stomped in after them and beckoned Meg outside. She obeyed, looking startled, and he confronted her angrily.

'Someone's been talking!' he said.

'I don't know what you mean!' she returned coldly.

'You know jolly well what I mean! . . . Someone's been and talked about – about last Saturday!'

'I haven't said a word.'

'Well, Gary Travers knows, anyway. Someone's been opening their big mouths!'

Tessa joined them. 'We haven't told anyone . . . Well, not anyone who couldn't be trusted,' she amended.

'You *have* been talking, then! I might have known!'

'The only people I've told were Melanie and David,' she said. 'They're friends of mine. I can trust them.'

'You obviously can't, then!'

'It wasn't them!' Tessa said, white-faced.

'It wasn't any of us,' Meg added. She looked at her brother and relented suddenly. 'You should know I wouldn't do a thing like that!' she told him reproachfully.

'That's the trouble, I don't know anything any more. Not now that you and she have got so taken up with each other!' he burst out, glaring at Tessa.

It was the wrong thing to have said, of course. Meg's eyes narrowed. 'Well, it was your own silly fault, wasn't it?' she shrugged.

He coloured. 'Thanks! I thought I could have relied on you, Meg, but obviously not any longer!'

His sister sighed. Until that fateful evening last weekend she would have stuck by her brother come what may. Now, suddenly, everything had changed. She thought of Gary Travers and his friends. 'They'll soon forget about it,' she said.

'And until then I'll be a laughing-stock!' he told her.

He turned away and went out into the garden. The torrential rain had changed to a fine drizzle but it was still misty and cold with lowering clouds scudding across a leaden sky. He kicked a football about until lunch-time, pondering on the events of the last few days. He thought of Sunday's picnic and remembered the twins sitting whispering and giggling in the front row. . . .

Peter and Paula were most likely to be the culprits, he decided. He'd tear strips off them when he saw them. . . .

* * *

The atmosphere at lunch-time was strained. Tessa and Meg spoke to each other only in undertones; Nick's appetite had gone and he sat in a morose silence pushing his food around his plate. He escaped as soon as he could.

Later, when he set out for the museum, he found to his considerable surprise that the two girls were waiting for him by the gate.

'Thought we might as well go along together,' Tessa said.

'Thank goodness it's almost stopped raining!' Meg murmured.

Nick grunted; they'd obviously decided to try and patch things up . . . Why couldn't they leave him alone? he asked himself; putting on an act, trying to impress him . . . It wouldn't wash with him, though; he was absolutely fed up with the lot of them!

Steve and a group of the children were waiting at the gate of the museum when they arrived; others soon joined them. Steve did a quick count. 'Twenty-four!' he announced. 'Go through all of you and I'll get the tickets.'

They did as they were told, but Nick lingered. He looked intently along the road that led to the camp-site. 'Twenty-five!' he amended as the tall figure of Chris came striding into view.

'I'll wait for him,' Steve said, and Nick went through the turnstile after the others.

There was still a fine drizzle falling; everyone was glad to get out of their wet anoraks. Nick's mood had lifted;

he was feeling more optimistic again.

There was plenty to look at — stuffed birds in cages, artifacts taken from wrecks, old prints and pictures, Roman coins and other memorabilia. It wasn't really his cup of tea, but Chris appeared to be enjoying himself.

If Nick had hoped to get into conversation with him, however, he was doomed to disappointment. The lone camper was clearly avoiding him still and managed to do so for the entire afternoon.

The visit to the museum hadn't been entirely fruitless, though. As soon as he got home, Nick searched in the pocket of his jeans for the piece of paper he had picked up off the floor of the museum. It was a shopping list and it had dropped out of one of Chris's pockets as he searched for his handkerchief.

He went to the dressing-table drawer and got out the other piece of paper — the one Melanie had found in the ruined cottage. He compared the two — the writing was identical!

Chapter 9

A Fishing Trip

The fine weather had returned by the next morning.

'How about a fishing trip today?' Bob MacLaren asked at breakfast time.

They all thought it a good idea.

'Right then! Two o'clock prompt at the quay!'

'Will we see any seals, Uncle?' Meg wanted to know.

'Very likely! There are usually quite a lot around the reef.'

Golden Spray was waiting at the bottom of the steps when the children arrived at the harbour. Bob MacLaren had gone on ahead and was already there with Badger. They all got aboard and Tessa took up her position beside her father at the helm.

'Can I steer later, please, Dad?' she asked.

'When we get further out,' he said, and they were off. Once out beyond the harbour the launch started to pitch and roll. Badger, balanced foursquare, sniffed appreciatively at the salty air.

The island lay ahead. Nick stood in the stern slightly apart from the others; he studied it intently as they passed it on their port side. The twins looked at each other and Tessa glanced at Meg. Her cousin had told her about Nick's second visit to the cottage on Sunday. His interest in Whale Island had obviously not lessened.

They left the island behind and headed out towards the reef. It stretched in a long unbroken line from east to west, soaring to several hundred feet in places. The sea rose and fell restlessly along its base.

'It's completely blotted out by spray in rough weather,' Bob MacLaren told them. Nick looked at it speculatively.

'You can take over now, Tessa; I'll get the fishing tackle organised,' her father told her presently. 'We'll go out a bit further; keep her well over to the right, though, away from the current. There should be good fishing out there!' and he pointed to a spot to the south-west of the reef.

Tessa took the wheel whilst her father disappeared below deck. He was up again soon with an armful of fishing-lines.

'One for each of you,' he said, doling them out. He demonstrated how they should be held. 'Not too tightly – you must be able to feel when the fish bite. Not too loosely; you might lose the lot – hook, line and sinker!'

Tessa steered *Golden Spray* a bit further out, then her father took over and she joined the others. They were all quiet, kneeling up around the sides of the launch staring intently at the water. The launch rocked gently at anchor, the sun poured down on them. When nothing had happened after twenty minutes they began to get restless.

'Not much around today!' Tessa said disappointedly.

'It's like that sometimes,' her father said. Next minute there was a shout from Peter.

'Oops! I've had a bite!' he yelled.

'Pull her in then!' his father instructed. 'Steady there, not so fast!'

Peter slowed down, hauling in hand over hand like a seasoned fisherman. Everyone held their breath as something silver streaked through the water. All of them, even Badger, leant forward in keen anticipation. There was no fish on the end though, only the silver hook. There were groans from Peter and shouts of laughter from the others.

'Ever been had?' Tessa chuckled.

Peter looked shattered. 'There *was* something there, I felt it!' he said indignantly.

'The fish that got away!' his father grinned. 'Never mind, son, better luck next time!'

They settled down again. Nick, at the other end of the

boat, was the next to feel a tug; he hauled his line in with obvious difficulty. 'Got a whale there, I should think!' his uncle quipped.

'Like Gary Travers!' Meg said, remembering.

'Whatever is it?' Paula gasped, leaning far out over the boat. Next moment an enormous piece of timber about three feet long appeared; it was seaweed-covered and encrusted with barnacles. Everybody looked in amazement; Tessa began to laugh.

'He's got something all right!' she chortled, and peals of merriment erupted. Nick was not amused; he released his 'catch', hurling it back into the water with a scowl. It went in like a torpedo in a flurry of spray.

'Part of a wreck, I should think,' his uncle said wryly. His nephew flung his line in again without speaking.

They waited another ten minutes; despondency settled in again. Then suddenly everything started to happen! First Tessa pulled in a fair-sized mackerel, then it was Meg's turn. Bob MacLaren removed the hooks from the unfortunate creatures' gullets and they flapped disconsolately on the deck. Badger sniffed the air and wagged his tail. Two minutes later Nick began hauling on his line again; once more he appeared to be having difficulty.

'What you got this time, then, half a house?' Peter tittered.

His cousin didn't answer. In a moment something large and silvery flashed through the water; it glinted in the sunshine as it rose to the surface. Nick hauled in his catch with a triumphant flourish and everybody looked at it as it flapped around the deck.

'An outsize pollock!' his uncle announced. 'Well done, son!' He removed the hook from the fish's throat and the children continued their vigil with renewed interest. The mackerel came thick and fast then. By the end of an hour and a half Tessa and Nick had four apiece, Meg had three, and the twins two each.

'That's enough for one day, I think! We'll go and look

for sea-birds and seals now,' Bob MacLaren said. He started the engine again and they chugged nearer the reef. The current ran quite fiercely at this point and they had to go out wide to avoid it. As the rugged outcrop drew nearer they saw that it was covered with myriads of sea-birds.

'Which are they?' Meg wanted to know, remembering the stuffed ones they had seen in the museum the previous afternoon.

'Cormorants and guillemots mostly – some shags too,' her uncle told her. 'Have a look through the binoculars.'

'What's the difference between shags and cormorants again?' Paula asked.

'Cormorants have white necks, shags have crests on their heads,' Tessa reminded her.

'Guillemots and razorbills both have white fronts, but razorbills have thicker necks and bills than guillemots,' Bob MacLaren added.

He took them in right up to the granite rocks; they towered high above their heads as *Golden Spray* rose gently on the swell. They took it in turns to use the binoculars. Meg produced her camera and tried to take some close-ups.

Suddenly Peter gave a shout and pointed; there on a big flat rock a huge grey creature with snout and whiskers basked in the sunshine. A couple of large soulful eyes watched them warily.

'A seal!' shouted Paula, nearly falling overboard.

'Don't shout, you'll frighten him!' Tessa warned, but she was too late. The bull seal heaved himself up on his four flippers, then slithered into the water with a splash. He eyed them from a safe distance as he bobbed about on the surface, just his head showing.

'There should be more further over,' Bob MacLaren said as they chugged on along the length of the reef.

'*Look!*' Meg gasped presently. 'Hundreds of them!' She reached for her camera again. The children crowded to the edge of the boat, taking turns with the binoculars. Seals of all sizes, including babies with snow-white coats, basked on the rocks.

'Aren't they gorgeous!' Meg said.

'They're great!' Tessa agreed.

They cruised around for nearly an hour looking at the seals. Whenever *Golden Spray* went in too close they slid off the rocks into the sea, floating gently to the rhythm of the swell, just their heads visible.

'They're as interested in us as we are in them,' Meg said.

'Relieves the monotony to have visitors, I expect,' Tessa laughed.

'We'll have to be going back now,' Bob MacLaren said at last. 'It's nearly five.'

'Can we come out here again?' Meg asked as he started up the engine.

'Next week, if you like,' he agreed.

They took a last look at the seals before they turned and headed for the mainland.

'They're most intelligent creatures,' Bob MacLaren said. 'Its sad that so many have died from pollution!'

'It's the same with the sea-birds when they get oiled, isn't it, Dad?' Tessa observed.

'I'm afraid so. They're doomed to die unless someone rescues them and cleans them up.'

They chugged on: the island lay ahead. Nick stood silent and alert again and Tessa and Meg exchanged glances. Soon it lay off to starboard.

Suddenly a strangled exclamation escaped Nick. He grabbed the binoculars and directed them towards a prehistoric standing stone situated just above the landing-stage. Meg remembered seeing it on the afternoon of the picnic.

'What's the matter?' she asked curiously, following the direction of his gaze.

'A ghost!' Paula murmured with a giggle.

If Nick heard he gave no sign; he continued staring fixedly through the binoculars. Only when the standing stone was no longer visible and they were sailing past the

Suddenly a strangled exclamation escaped Nick

island's western shore, did he speak. 'There is someone on the island,' he said slowly. 'Someone who doesn't want to be seen!'

His uncle gave him a long, searching look. 'What makes you think that, lad?'

'He dodged behind that big stone when he saw me looking.'

Tessa and Meg exchanged glances; Tessa decided he needed humouring. 'What was he like?' she asked.

Her cousin didn't answer; he knew who he thought he looked like but none of them would believe him! The only sounds to be heard were the chug-chug of the engine and the swish of the sea against the sides of the boat.

'Spooks!' Peter muttered and Paula started to giggle.

'Shut up!' Tessa whispered. She looked at Meg, trying to hide a smile, then glanced at her father. Bob MacLaren was staring straight ahead of him towards the mainland.

'People don't often land,' he said quietly. 'Even if there *was* someone, anyone can go there, you know. I think you're letting your imagination run away with you, lad.'

Nick went white. 'I tell you, there's something funny going on,' he insisted fiercely, his eyes still on the island fast receding into the distance. Nobody spoke, and a cloud passed across the sky at that moment, blotting out the sunshine.

Five minutes later they entered the harbour; Nick was still looking pale. As his uncle steered a path between the motley craft floating on its oily surface, an angry light shone in his eyes.

They reached the harbour steps; Meg was the first to break the silence. 'Thanks for a lovely afternoon, Uncle!' she said.

'Glad you've enjoyed it,' he smiled. He secured the launch and busied himself stringing the fish together in two neat bunches.

'Fourteen mackerel and one pollock!' he announced. Who's going to carry them?'

'We will!' shouted the twins, and ran up the steps with

their trophy. At that moment the cloud passed over and the sun came out again. Tessa and Meg followed with Badger; the two girls were talking and laughing as though nothing out of the ordinary had occurred.

'A nice surprise for Mum,' Tessa said as they set off along the road. 'I'm looking forward to my supper!'

'Me too!' Meg said.

Nick followed at a distance. They could think what they liked, he told himself. He'd show 'em!

Chapter 10

Nick's Plan

In spite of his resolution, Nick found the next few days trying. He overheard Tessa talking about his 'crazy fixation', as she called it – she obviously thought he was going round the twist! – whilst the twins' thinly-veiled comments left him in no doubt as to their opinion of him. As for Uncle Bob and Aunt Jane, they shook their heads and sighed almost every time they looked at him.

In the end he took to wandering off on his own for hours at a time. It was no good trying to explain to anybody; they would never accept that Chris could be mixed up in anything shady. He went to church on Sundays, and joined in with the club's activities. That was it as far as they were concerned!

It wasn't as if there was anyone he could talk things over with – not now that Meg had defected to the enemy. He would never have believed that she could have got herself so involved! There was Melanie, of course; Melanie didn't make snide remarks and poke fun. She, too, was well in with the gang, though, as he called it, and he wasn't sure how far he could trust her either.

Chris was up to no good, of that he was convinced. He knew now that he had been on the island; comparing the scraps of paper Melanie had found in the cottage with the shopping list he had dropped in the museum had convinced him of that – if he needed any convincing! He was ninety-nine per cent certain he had been there on the day of the fishing trip, too! Remembering his first meeting with Chris right at the beginning of the holiday, he had made a point of walking along the cliff-top late in the evening whenever possible, in the hope of catching him either going over to the island or coming back. So far he hadn't had any luck; Chris was undoubtedly being extra careful not to be seen.

In the end he decided to go to the camp-site again and try to get into conversation. He didn't fancy his chances, though; the lone camper was slippery and not easy to pin down. As it turned out, however, his opportunity came sooner than he had expected. He was sauntering along the lane leading up from Kennet Sands just before lunch a couple of days later when a tall figure swung into view ahead, wending his way down the road that led to the camp-site. Without stopping to think, Nick hurried after him.

'Hi! Been out to the island yet?' he sang out as he caught up with the object of his meditations.

'Couldn't manage the trip with the club the other Sunday,' the lone camper told him after a moment's hesitation.

'Pity – you should go sometime!' Nick said, a glint in his eye.

'Didn't think people normally landed,' his companion returned innocently.

'You can do if you get hold of a boat.'

'Or swim!' Chris remarked after a short pause.

Nick frowned and bit his lip; he hadn't expected that! Before he could think up an appropriate reply they were at the entrance to the camp-site. Chris turned in at the gate; he obviously had no intention of hanging around. 'Cheerio!' he said breezily.

Nick's hackles rose; he wasn't letting him get away with that! 'Do you know the island's haunted?' he called after him.

Chris swung round; there was an unfathomable expression in the steady grey eyes.

'I should keep away from the island if I were you,' he said evenly.

Nick was silent, dumbstruck. By the time he had

gathered his scattered wits Chris was gone, striding off towards the small brown tent pitched slightly apart from the others. Had there been a veiled threat in those smoothly-spoken words? Nick asked himself as he followed him with his blue eyes. He stood pondering for a moment; then, feeling hungry, and remembering that it must be nearly lunch-time, he set off at a trot in the direction of the guest-house.

One thing was certain, he told himself as he went along, Chris had an interest in the island, too. But what was it? There was only one way to find out, he decided grimly, and that was to go over there again and catch him red-handed at whatever it was he was up to!

Having mulled the matter over some more during the afternoon, he eventually decided that the best time to make the trip would be the following Saturday. A session of beach games had been arranged and a picnic tea, so nobody would miss him, not even Tessa and Meg, who he had a shrewd suspicion, had been told off to keep watch on him. Due to the state of the tides which were particularly high at the moment, another beach a mile or two up the coast had been chosen instead of Kennet Sands. That would suit him fine, he told himself; he would be able to get away in old Bill's rowing-boat without any problem.

On the Friday afternoon he strolled over to the beach to reconnoitre. The little rowing-boat *Seagull* was in the hollow between the two sand-dunes where she always lay. He looked at her thoughtfully, he was certain he could handle her. If Chris wasn't at the camp-site and didn't turn up for the picnic the next day, the chances were he would be on the island! Already he was beginning to savour the delights of telling Tessa and the rest – particularly Tessa whom he considered too cocky by far – that he wasn't as daft as he appeared!

As it happened things didn't turn out quite to plan. In the first place the weather forecast on the Friday evening wasn't too good. A break in the long hot spell of dry weather was predicted, with rain and storms sweeping in across the Atlantic and even possible outbreaks of thunder. Because of this, and unbeknown to Nick, the venue for the picnic had been changed at the last minute; access to the other beach was difficult in bad weather due to there being a long slippery pathway down the steep cliff. The children were to meet at Kennet Sands after all!

Nick himself didn't get to hear about the change of plan because, as he frequently grumbled to himself, no one ever told him anything nowadays. Consequently, when he arrived at the beach soon after lunch the next day intent on launching the rowing-boat and making a speedy get-away, he discovered to his dismay that Uncle Bob, David, Tessa and Meg, along with some of the rest of the gang, were there. The little rowing-boat was still sitting amongst the sand-dunes, but what use was that to him? he asked himself, perplexed. He'd never be able to push it down to the sea, row away under the very nose of the enemy, and get away with it. To make matters worse the promised change in the weather had arrived with a vengeance; it was much cooler, with a grey cloudy sky reflected in an even dingier grey sea.

If only he had known about the new arrangements, he thought drearily, surveying the unpromising scene and his uncle, Tessa and Meg from behind a sand-dune. Then he could have slipped out immediately after breakfast and been home and dry by now.

It didn't take him long to dream up an alternative scheme, however. He had to get a rowing-boat from somewhere, and whose better than Tessa's? He had already ascertained that Chris wasn't at the camp-site; now he had to make sure that he didn't turn up for the beach games. When by a quarter to three there was no sign of him, he ducked low amongst the spiky marram grass in an effort to make himself as inconspicuous as possible and crawled on hands and knees towards the cliff path. Away from the beach he set off at a run towards the harbour.

There were quite a lot of holiday-makers milling around on the quay when he got there, driven off the beaches by

He slipped over to the harbour wall and peered down

the bad weather. He slipped over to the harbour wall and peered down; a couple of brightly painted dinghies, one orange, one red, were moored at the bottom of the steps. There was absolutely no sign of a blue one, though, and with a stab of disappointment he suddenly remembered that Tessa's boat, *Puffin*, was in dock for a repaint. He looked at the two dinghies at the bottom of the steps again. He'd never get away in one of those, he told himself – the owners were probably around and would see him.

He stared around for further inspiration and remembered the small, rarely-used jetty at the other end of the quay. He hurried towards it and noticed a small black rowing-boat bobbing about on the oily water. With a swift glance round to make sure no one was looking he sped quickly down the uneven, seaweed-covered steps. At the bottom he looked up and jumped, startled! A couple of policemen were standing on the jetty looking down; he was certain they had their eye on him!

'Just my luck!' he muttered, coming over a bit shaky, and decided to hang around a moment longer as though admiring the scenery. Then he turned and walked quickly back up the steps again. Getting a boat from the harbour was turning out to be a useless idea.

He strolled moodily back through the town and as he did so he saw another couple of policemen. There were a lot of bobbies about this afternoon; did they know about his plan to pinch a boat? he wondered. That was ridiculous, though, he decided; it was only his guilty conscience!

Another idea occurred to him and he drew a quick breath and stopped dead in his tracks. When eventually he walked on again there was a spring in his step and a light in his eye. He was more than ever determined to make the crossing to the island!

*   *   *

A game of cricket was in full swing when he got back to Kennet Sands; he went straight to the hollow in the dunes for another reassuring look at the boat. There was no chance of getting away yet though . . . to his dismay Meg and Tessa were standing not a hundred yards away, fielding. He ducked out of sight and looked up at the sky. A heavy bank of cloud was building up on the horizon and a stiffish breeze had sprung up.

Forgetting caution he got to his feet and at that very moment Tessa glanced round and saw him. To his surprise, she gave him a wave and a friendly smile.

'Hi there, Nick! Where did you spring from?' she shouted.

Meg looked round too. 'Oh, hello, Nick!' she said, and sounded quite pleased to see him for a change.

Then Melanie spotted him. 'Are you going to join us?' she asked with a smile.

'Yes, do!' Tessa said.

Nick, secretly flattered, eyed them suspiciously. *Now* what were they up to, he asked himself, and why had they chosen such an inconvenient moment to be so welcoming? Join in? Well, right now he hadn't much choice, had he? He'd just have to stay and make the best of it for a while; after that, he'd be on his way! He looked quickly around to see if Chris had turned up but there was no sign of him.

So he stood where Tessa told him to, and at the end of twenty minutes he was almost beginning to enjoy himself. He wielded the cricket bat with enthusiasm, sending the ball flying far out over the water. Life wasn't so bad after all, he decided. It was like old times with Tessa and Meg talking again. By the time they broke off for tea he'd almost convinced himself that rowing out to the island was a stupid idea, for this afternoon at any rate. He'd go another time.

Unfortunately something happened a couple of minutes later that made him change his mind. He was talking to Melanie and munching a sardine sandwich when Gary Travers happened to look in his direction and their eyes met. 'Hello, Nick!' he yelled. 'Seen any ghosts lately?'

Some of the younger kids, Peter and Paula included,

started to giggle. Melanie bit her lip and Tessa looked at Meg. As for Nick, all the aggro came surging back. He clenched his fists, turned pale and glared across the beach at his adversary. That had done it, he told himself; he'd be off to the island as soon as he could get away!

That wasn't to be yet, though. When all the food and squash was finished, some of the children started kicking a beach ball around and the younger ones began a game of hopscotch. Nick ignored Tessa, Meg and Melanie and wandered off down to the tide-line where he stood chucking pebbles. Storm clouds were gathering out to sea and a stiffish breeze had sprung up, ruffling the surface of the ocean. Why couldn't they hurry up and go? he asked himself exasperatedly.

When he turned round next Melanie was passing song-books round and everybody was sitting down. Nick went and joined them because he didn't have much alternative. It would pass the time, anyway! Tessa and Meg came and seated themselves one on either side of him so that he felt like a prisoner; they were still going out of their way to be pleasant. Baffled by his sudden unexpected return to favour, he looked perplexedly at the song-book Melanie had handed him.

Someone chose a chorus and they started to sing. Nick kept his mouth firmly closed, however, and glowered over to where Gary Travers was sitting on the edge of the crowd, busy throwing sand over his cronies. After a few more songs, Uncle Bob started talking about Jonah being swallowed by a big fish and his nephew listened cynically with half an ear. Only when his uncle went on to say that there had been other instances of people being swallowed by whales and surviving, did he become mildly interested.

They sung more choruses, then it was time to go. The three girls were still hovering around him and Nick was beginning to feel more like his old self once more. Again he decided to postpone his island trip to a more auspicious occasion; he would go back home with the others! The children started to drift off in twos and threes, all except

Tessa, Meg and Melanie. It was obvious they wished to call a truce.

'Glad you came, Nick!' Tessa murmured.

'Smashing!' Meg said awkwardly.

Peter and Paula ran up at that moment. 'Great, wasn't it?' they chorused, overdoing it a bit.

Nick glowered at them.

'Go home, twins!' Tessa said quickly, and looked at her cousin again. 'Are you coming back with us, Nick?' she asked.

'Come on, Nick !' Melanie pleaded.

He looked at her and wavered but at that moment Gary Travers returned for his beach ball. He caught Nick's eye again and smirked and all Nick's resentment came surging back.

'You go on; I'll catch you up in a minute,' he said abruptly.

'Er – all right,' Meg murmured uncertainly.

Tessa bit her lip. 'See you later then, Nick,' she said, looking a bit crestfallen.

'In church tomorrow?' Melanie asked hopefully.

'Er . . . yes, OK,' he said.

They walked away, leaving him on his own. He sighed, for the fibs had just slipped out; he certainly wasn't going back yet and he had no intention of being in church tomorrow. . . .

Melanie's voice, louder than she'd intended, wafted back to him on the breeze. 'We're supposed to be Christians! We'll never get him to come to things and join in with us if we don't . . .'

'We've tried to be friendly; we can't do any more.' It was Tessa this time.

'If he wants to be like that . . .' Meg said, but the remainder of the sentence was lost to Nick.

With a final glance in his direction, the three girls set off slowly in the wake of the others, and Nick turned towards the boat in the sand-dunes.

Chapter 11

Nick in Trouble Again

As soon as the last of the beach party had disappeared from sight along the cliff path Nick sprang into action. With a stealthy look in all directions to see that there was no one about, he picked up the rope attached to the painter of *Seagull* and started hauling the little craft down to the tideline. He hadn't far to go; the tide was well up by now. It was a somewhat hazardous undertaking as well he knew, for he was in full view of anybody who might chance to walk along the cliff path. That was a risk he would have to take, though, he told himself.

He was soon down at the water's edge and pushing *Seagull* out on to the waves. He hung on to her as she bobbed up and down on top of the water. Whale Island looked an awfully long way off and something inside him warned him to give up his hair-brained scheme and go home. At the same time another voice urged him on, and remembering all he'd had to put up with over the past weeks he hesitated only a second. With a final glance all round he climbed into the boat and started to row.

It was a good thing, he reflected, he'd had that practice in *Puffin* the other day; at least he knew how to handle a rowing-boat! He tried to feather his oars as Tessa had shown him, but it wasn't as easy on the sea as in the harbour; the water was quite choppy and he kept shipping crabs.

He pressed on, however, and hadn't gone far when he thought he detected a movement amongst the sand-dunes. Was someone watching him? he asked himself. He continued looking, but whoever it was had disappeared. Had it been Chris? he wondered. Somehow he didn't think so, for something told him the lone camper was on the island . . .

He was getting on quite well, making reasonable headway, when he heard the first rumble of thunder. It sounded a long way off, though, and he wasn't too worried. A few minutes later, however, a flash of lightning lit the sky, followed after a brief pause by another rumble, louder this time. The storm was drawing nearer!

He rowed on. The sky grew dark and threatening; raindrops spattered down on him and the sea started to toss and churn. The waves were growing bigger; angry-looking breakers rolled towards him on all sides. With mounting panic Nick realised he was making little or no progress. The island was almost invisible, lost in the mist, and he had a horrible idea he was completely off course.

He peered about in the rising storm for a familiar landmark. He was struggling now; waves slapped against the sides of the boat, white horses, foam-flecked and angry. Everywhere he looked, menacing black rocks reared their ugly heads; they lay on all sides, the sea rising and falling around them. He began to lose all sense of direction; when he peered back towards where he thought the shore ought to be, it too had disappeared, blotted out by the fog.

Another flash of lightning lit the sky, a crash sounded immediately overhead. The storm was on him! With several inches of water already filling the bottom of the boat and nothing to bail it out with, progress was almost down to nil. He'd better try to make for the harbour, he told himself through clenched teeth, but where was the harbour?

He tried to turn the boat around, but the tide was running out quite strongly now and defied all his efforts. *Seagull* juddered alarmingly, waves crashed around the rocks sending up spume and spray. Fingers blistered and painful, Nick fought with the creaking oars. The rain sheeted down on him, it stung his face, his bare arms and legs.

Suddenly Nick's tormented mind winged back to the story Uncle Bob had told them on the beach only an hour or so ago – was it really only an hour? It seemed like centuries . . . He remembered it clearly; it was about Jonah, the prophet in the Old Testament. Jonah had been told by God to go and preach to some people he didn't want to preach to. So what did he do? He ran away! Was he running away from God, too? Nick asked himself – for he was quite certain by now that God was out there somewhere . . . Was this his punishment, and if so what could he do about it, out here in a storm and about to drown?

There *was* one thing he could do, he remembered; he could pray. He hadn't prayed properly for ages, not since he was a kid. Now he found himself saying in a trembly voice, 'P-please, *please*, God! Forgive me for running away from You; for doing my own thing and taking *Seagull* without asking. P-please, *please* h-help m-me to get back to l-land!'

Forked lightning streaked across the sky at that moment, worse than any that had gone before; a crashing roar rumbled and reverberated around the heavens. God must be very angry with him indeed, Nick decided, and as he wasn't likely to be swallowed by a big fish, he would in all probability sink to the bottom of the ocean and that would be that!

Whilst these thoughts chased themselves through his bemused brain, his efforts to keep the boat going were becoming feebler and feebler. His T-shirt and shorts were sodden, he was chilled to the bone. Quaking in every limb, he became suddenly aware of something large and dark looming up to starboard. He peered at it through the mist and driving rain and realised with a great surge of relief that it wasn't just another rock, it was too big for that . . . Perhaps it was the mainland!

He was quite near to it now; he could see it clearly. It

wasn't the mainland, though, but a small rocky island with a little sandy beach. At the same time he was conscious of a lull in the storm and of the wind blowing less forcefully. Instead of tossing around like a pea in a saucepan of boiling water, the dinghy was drifting in a sort of lagoon parallel with the shore, carried high on the long smooth rollers. He was in the lee of an island, sheltered from the worst of the storm.

He shipped his oars, searching for a suitable place to land. It was then that he saw what appeared to be a small building amongst the trees, just distinguishable through the mist and driving rain. As he looked at it, something clicked; this was the eastern side of Whale Island and he was looking at the ruined cottage. He had arrived!

It was difficult to see in the half-light; he rubbed his eyes and scanned the beach. He must get ashore somehow though it wasn't going to be easy. A large wave rolled towards him and he awaited it; with any luck it would carry him ashore broadside on. It swept on, leaving him behind and almost capsizing him. He tried again with the next breaker, but the same thing happened; each time he attempted to ride in on a wave, *Seagull* almost overturned in a flurry of froth and foam. He tried standing up in the boat, digging one oar into the sand and shoving against it in an effort to bring the dinghy up on to the shore. Then, just he was making some slight progress, he happened to glance towards the cottage. As a flash of lightning lit the scene he saw something that filled him with total horror.

Someone – or something – was standing at the top of the beach; it was coming towards him, gesticulating wildly – a ghostly white-faced object waving its arms and apparently mouthing threats. For a long moment Nick stood petrified in the middle of the boat; then, galvanised into action and not waiting to discover more, he fell sprawling onto his backside, seized the other oar and turned and rowed off as though in training for the Olympics. Better to drown, he told himself through chattering teeth, than to share the island with a ghost!

With no idea where he was going, he went blindly on, intent only on putting as much distance as he could between himself and the island. The sea churned less wildly now for the storm was moving further away; though lightning still forked across the sky and thunder rolled intermittently.

He hadn't gone far when he was suddenly aware of no longer having to battle against the waves; of being borne swiftly along without any effort on his part. He looked at the inky black water swirling around the boat and he remembered the current. That was it, he realised, he was caught in the current again!

The fog had lifted somewhat, and stupefied by the trauma of it all he looked ahead to where he thought the horizon ought to be. He couldn't see it, but there *was* something out there, something almost obliterated by spray – a long line of black jagged rocks that stretched from east to west in an unbroken line.

His dulled senses came unfrozen at that moment, the truth dawned. It was the reef he was looking at – no longer calm and serene as it had been on the day they had gone looking for seals, but wild and menacing.

His thoughts went back to the first evening of the holiday; he remembered what the twins had said about the reef. 'Deadmen's Teeth' they had called it, for it was deadly; ships had foundered on the reef, thousands of them!

With a sudden, sickening sense of impending doom, Nick realised that the current was carrying him straight towards the reef. The boat was about to be broken up on it, and him with it . . .

Chapter 12
The Search

Nick's departure in the rowing-boat earlier in the evening had not, in fact, gone undetected. Police Sergeant Perkins chanced to be out patrolling the cliffs and arrived at Kennet Sands just as Nick was dragging *Seagull* down to the water's edge. The Sergeant was almost entirely hidden from him by a tall sand-dune, however, and as he jumped aboard the dinghy and fitted the oars into the rowlocks, Nick had no idea that he was under observation.

'Old Bill Fletcher's boat!' the Sergeant said aloud. 'The old chap must have given him permission to go for a spin round the bay.' He watched as the young oarsman pulled away from the shore; he wasn't near enough to be certain but he thought he looked very much like Bob MacLaren's nephew.

That reminded him that it had been young MacLaren who had nearly gone and got himself drowned in that silly attempt to swim out to the island. The lad had seemed to have mended his ways since then, though; his sister was very much involved with Tessa MacLaren and the church youth club, so it must be all right!

'Could have chosen a better day, though!' he muttered, glancing up at the sky.

Nick was getting into his stride now; the boy appeared to be handling the boat quite competently. It wouldn't hurt to give him a shout, though, the Sergeant told himself. He cupped his hands to his mouth and yelled, 'Ahoy there!' but there was a stiffish breeze blowing off the sea and he might just as well have saved his breath. Nick

MacLaren rowed on undisturbed.

With a final look, and making up his mind to pop in at Bill Fletcher's later on to check, Sergeant Perkins left the beach. He had more important things on his mind, however, and he promptly forgot! By a coincidence, just as he was about to enter the little police station some twenty minutes later, who should he bump into but old Bill himself.

'Hello there!' wheezed the latter. 'Bit o' rough weather coming up, by the looks o' things!'

Sergeant Perkins raised his eyes to the threatening sky and nodded. 'It does that, Bill; it'll clear the air, anyway.'

'Aye, bin mighty hot these last few days. Thought as summat would 'appen to break it up!'

Sergeant Perkins remembered the boy with the rowing-boat at Kennet Sands. 'Saw someone who looked like Bob MacLaren's nephew from the guest-house up top o' hill,' he went on casually, 'taking your rowing-boat out into the bay. S'pose you gave him permission, eh?'

'Takin' me rowing-boat out in the bay! Young MacLaren!' he spluttered. 'Hindeed I didn't give 'im permission!' He fretted and fumed and Sergeant Perkins became anxious; the old chap seemed in imminent danger of bursting a blood vessel. Looked as though he'd got himself a few more problems letting the boy go off like that!

'I'd better get back there . . .' he began, but Bill interrupted. 'Just because young Tessa borrowed it that night the stupid boy swam out to the island, there's no reason for 'im to think 'e can do likewise! Give him permission indeed, the very idea! . . . If there's any damage . . .'

Sergeant Perkins sighed. After the fiasco of a little while back he'd have thought the young blighter would have learnt his lesson. He really ought to have checked, and under normal circumstances he would have done so.

'I'd better get back to the beach straight away,' he muttered. 'With this weather coming up . . .'

'You should have stopped 'im!' growled old Bill. 'Can't think why you didn't after what 'appened!'

The policeman looked embarrassed. 'I've just got to nip into the station to report, then I'll be with you. We've got a spot of bother on our hands at the moment,' he added by way of excuse.

'You'll have a spot more bother soon,' old Bill grumbled, glaring after the arm of the law's retreating figure. He stamped around on the pavement, muttering to himself, but he didn't have long to wait. In a moment the door reopened and the Sergeant emerged.

'Come on, let's get going then,' Perkins said. 'The boy would surely have more sense than to . . .'

'Sense! He's got about as much sense as a cabbage!' Bill snorted.

Perkins grunted. They set off, the older man hobbling in the wake of the Sergeant as quickly as his 'rheumatics' would allow.

Storm clouds scudded across the sky as they plodded on. There came a flash of lightning followed by a distant peal of thunder. They climbed a stile and took a short cut across some fields; a fine drizzle had begun to fall.

They reached the beach and the Sergeant pointed to the spot where he had last sighted Nick. There was no sign of a boat, however – only a grey expanse of ocean with not a vessel in sight. At that moment another flash of lightning lit the sky, followed shortly afterwards by a crashing roll. The storm was drawing nearer!

Old Bill frowned and peered down on to the beach. 'That's where I leave my dinghy . . . there!' he told Perkins, stabbing a stumpy forefinger in the direction of the hollow in the dunes. 'Only a couple of minutes from my cottage and 'andy for seeing to me lobster-pots . . . What am I going to do without me ole boat?' he whined.

'No sign of him, absolutely no sign!' mumbled the Sergeant under his breath. As if he hadn't got enough on his plate without this. He hunched his shoulders and looked up at the sky. If young MacLaren was out in the rowing-boat with a storm about to launch itself, though, something must be done about it, and quickly. It wasn't only the boat that was in danger, though anyone would have thought so the way the old chap was carrying on. 'I'll get back to the harbour and take a launch out for a scout round,' he said resignedly.

'And I'll come along with 'ee,' old Bill told him grimly. 'Can't afford to lose me boat!'

The two men turned back in the direction of the town. It was raining heavily now. Lightning flashed intermittently and thunder rolled in the distance. A police launch, with two policemen on board shrouded in oilskins, lay moored at the bottom of the harbour steps when they arrived. Bill looked at it and frowned. He glanced curiously at the Sergeant, remembering what he had said earlier on. 'What's up, then?' he enquired.

The Sergeant said nothing. He sprinted down the steps and had a whispered consultation with his colleagues in the boat. Then he looked up to the top of the quay. 'We're going straight out to have a scout round, Bill!' he yelled. 'Want to come?'

'Aye, I'm not losing me rowing-boat, not if I knows anythin' about it!' and the old chap limped down towards the launch, stiff joints forgotten. When he was settled in the stern under a tarpaulin, Sergeant Perkins started up the engine and they were away.

They hugged the coast for ten minutes or so, heading back towards Kennet Sands, and passing the island. Thunder and lightning rumbled around as they scanned the sea in all directions, but there was no sign of a boy in a rowing-boat, and a disturbing thought occurred to the Sergeant. Nick might well have decided to pack it in when the storm started; he could have left the boat on another beach and gone home!

It was too late to say so now; he'd look ridiculous! Besides, the boy could well be out here and in danger. They'd better cruise around a while longer, then call it a day. He only hoped his companions wouldn't start asking awkward questions.

'I'll take her further out,' he said abruptly, and changed course.

Inspector Roberts exchanged a quick glance with Constable Collins. 'As you wish,' he shrugged.

Another flash of lightning sheeted across the sky, a deafening crash broke overhead. They passed Whale Island again, pitching and rolling on the breakers. As Perkins looked at it another idea occurred to him. 'I'd better suss out the island,' he said, turning the helm.

'OK,' murmured the Inspector, almost past caring.

They headed back, making for its southern shore. The little jetty came into view but there was no rowing-boat tied up. He'd better have a scout round all the same, Perkins decided; the place certainly seemed to hold a fascination for the boy. He brought the launch in with some difficulty and secured it. Then he jumped ashore.

'Won't be long!' he called, and sprinted across the sand.

In a few minutes he reached the cottage; he went round to the front and looked inside, and even as he did so he had the strong impression he was being watched. He cupped his hands to his mouth and yelled, 'Hello there!', but his voice was drowned by a crash of thunder immediately overhead. Water dripped down on him from the trees, forked lightning zig-zagged across the sky.

He stood pondering for a moment, and suddenly a startling thought leapt into his head. He stepped quickly out of the cottage; his eyes darted this way and that. There was nothing to be seen, however, and with a last wary look to right and left he walked rapidly away through the undergrowth. He'd have a quick look round the beaches before going back, he told himself, and did so, keenly on the alert. Should he tell his colleagues of his latest suspicion? he wondered. He decided to leave it for the moment and concentrate on the job in hand. They'd better sort young Nick out first!

'Er, nothing there!' he announced as he climbed on board the launch.

The Inspector grunted; he was beginning to feel seasick. They headed out again, on the crest of a wave one minute, down in a trough the next. Breakers pounded the launch, it creaked and groaned like a soul in torment. The men had a job to keep their feet as the sea poured across its deck – all except for old Bill crouched snugly under the tarpaulin!

Young MacLaren *had* to be at home, he'd just got to be, Sergeant Perkins told himself as the skies chucked rain down on them like water out of a bucket. He'd get into trouble for bringing them all out on this hopeless pursuit, but what of that?

Lightning zig-zagged across the heavens again, another crackle reverberated all around. Suddenly Inspector Roberts gave a shout. 'Over there to starboard, Perkins!' he yelled.

The Sergeant followed the Inspector's trembling finger and sucked in his breath, horrified. Constable Collins gasped.

Several hundred yards away a rowing-boat had appeared. It drifted oarless, tossed like a shuttlecock, visible one minute, the next lost from sight in the trough of a wave.

Chapter 13

A Near Thing!

'Great Scott!' murmured Inspector Roberts.

'Is there anyone in it?' breathed Collins.

The Inspector stared aghast. Next minute he saw a boy crouched in a huddle. 'In the current and heading straight for the reef!' he muttered.

There was a moment's silence before Perkins leapt into action. Nick's life was in deadly danger.

'Throw out the life-lines!' he shouted.

The Inspector and Collins leapt to obey. Old Bill, hearing the commotion, tottered out from under the tarpaulin; he followed the Sergeant's riveted gaze. 'Crazy little blighter!' he gasped, and shambled below deck after the others.

The men returned and ranged themselves on the fore-deck. Sergeant Perkins cupped his hands to his mouth and bawled to attract Nick's attention. Borne along by the current, tossed about like a cork, the boy in the rowing-boat appeared strangely indifferent to his surroundings.

'*Nick!*' he yelled again. There was no response. 'Come on, all together!' he urged.

They shouted in chorus. Nick's head turned in their direction. He saw the launch and raised an arm.

'Get ready!' Perkins yelled, and got into a crouching position, grasped the side of the launch with one hand and leant forward over the water. The ropes snaked out; each fell short by a few feet.

They tried again; this time they were nearer the mark. Not near enough, though, and the watchers on the launch groaned. Like Perkins, old Bill was only too well aware of the power of the current and the treachery of the reef. He shook his head despairingly, no longer concerned for the safety of his boat, but for the boy.

'Get in closer, Perkins!' urged the Inspector. The Sergeant eyed the swirling eddy; it was too near for comfort.

'Almost as close as we dare, Sir!' he returned hoarsely. 'We'll need help ourselves if we get into that lot!' He edged a bit further all the same; once more the ropes spiralled and fell short.

They were within a hundred yards of Nick now. He knelt sodden and terrified. They tried again and this time the Inspector's rope fell within reach. A gasp went up from the launch as the boy leant far out over the waves. *Seagull* almost capsized but he had hold of the rope with his right hand and a cheer went up.

'Hang on!' shouted the men and, miraculous as it seemed, he did. How long would he be able to keep it up, though? Suffering from cold and exposure, he looked all in.

With the Inspector, the Constable and old Bill ranged one behind the other, a tug-of-war followed. The men slipped and slithered on the wet deck whilst Sergeant Perkins exerted his strength to keep the launch steady. Could they suck the dinghy out of the whirlpool without being drawn into it themselves? – that was the vital question.

It seemed highly doubtful but they struggled on, oblivious of the returning storm. Sheet lightning mingled with the forked to light up the desperate scene. The minutes passed and a thick mist swept in, hanging shroud-like on the air. It blotted out both boy and boat and failure seemed inevitable as the launch moved inch by inch into the current . . .

The Sergeant eyed the black rocks not five hundred yards off and his stomach turned over. Next thing they were in the whirlpool!

They were within a hundred yards of Nick

'Hang on everyone!' he shouted. 'Let's hope and pray he can keep his hold, otherwise . . .'

He didn't finish the sentence. Old Bill was at his side. He looked at him. 'What be you goin' to do, Sir?' he breathed.

'Bring her round! Give me a hand, Bill!'

The old man braced himself against the wheel alongside the Sergeant. His 'rheumatics' were forgotten. The Inspector and Collins looked at the Sergeant. They weren't sure what was going on but it was up to him and the old chap now.

'Hang on, Nick!' yelled Perkins into the mist. 'Don't let go!'

'Hold tight!' shouted the Inspector and the Constable in chorus.

Perkins let out the throttle.

'Hard over now!' he breathed.

Bill did as he was told. He and Perkins prepared to do battle with the elements. Sweat poured off their faces and mingled with the rain. There was a singing noise in Perkins' ears.

Inch by inch, centimetre by centimetre the boat turned, swinging on its axis. Painfully, laboriously, with the two men leaning hard on the wheel, it was moving out of the whirling, eddying current to safety.

Another minute and they were free.

'The boy!' gasped a perspiring Perkins, relaxing his hold on the wheel. He looked over his shoulder.

'Hanging on, just about!' reassured the Inspector.

'Not for much longer, I should think!' muttered Collins.

Sergeant Perkins breathed again. The miracle had happened!

They weren't a second too soon, either. Once safely out of the current, Nick's frenzied grasp relaxed; his hold gave way. Slumped in a heap in the bottom of the rowing-boat, the superhuman strength given him when he needed it had ebbed away. Out of danger at last, he had fainted.

The rescue boat was soon alongside; willing hands leant

down to haul him to safety. Whilst Inspector Roberts and Constable Collins carried him down to the cabin, Bill leant over the side of the launch and lashed *Seagull* safely to it. He gave the dinghy a fond look. 'Me ole rowing-boat!' he murmured.

Nick was soon round again; he looked deathly pale. They found dry clothing in a locker and a few sips of hot chocolate brought a tinge of colour to his face. He lay still on his bunk bed, a sick feeling coming over him as he thought of his uncle. He must surely believe him this time though, when he told him what had happened at the island again this afternoon.

Meanwhile Sergeant Perkins went up on deck again and the launch rolled and tossed its way back to the harbour. By the time it got there the storm had blown itself out and a watery sun shone through the clouds. They carried Nick up the slippery steps on an improvised stretcher. All that remained now was to get him back to the guest-house; the sooner the better, too, for he looked pretty groggy. First, however, there was Bill to be thanked for his part in the rescue operation.

'All in a day's work!' the old man assured them modestly as he hobbled back down the steps to his rowing-boat. They watched him set off in the direction of Kennet Sands; then, with a shivering and subdued Nick in tow – he could walk that distance now, he told them – they made tracks for the police station.

'I'll run him straight back, Inspector,' said Perkins when they got there.

'OK, Sarge, see you!'

Sergeant Perkins piloted Nick towards a waiting police car.

*   *   *

Policeman and boy were silent on the way back to the guest-house. Neither felt in the mood for conversation, each was busy with his own thoughts. Perkins could visualise without too much difficulty Bob MacLaren's reaction when he discovered what Nick had been up to again; he wouldn't like to exchange places with the boy, he reflected grimly.

As for Nick, he had come to a momentous decision. At the risk of bringing down further anger and ridicule upon his head, he would tell Sergeant Perkins the whole story from beginning to end. He *must* believe him, he told himself desperately!

Chapter 14
Nick's Story

Sergeant Perkins drew to a halt outside the guest-house. Nick took a deep breath. His teeth were chattering so much he could hardly speak.

'I-I s-saw it again this afternoon, S-sir!' he began, but the Sergeant wasn't listening. The boy didn't look too good, he thought; maybe he needed a doctor. He hustled him out of the car and they walked up the path. Perkins rang the door-bell but there was no response. The MacLarens must be out searching.

Nick took the Sergeant round to the side entrance and they went into the kitchen. He was glad no one was in; anything to defer the dreadful moment when he had to face his uncle. It was a good chance for him to say what he had to say to the Sergeant, too. He sank down on a chair and took a deep breath.

'I-I saw it again this afternoon, Sir!' he repeated in a low tense voice. 'S-same as I did before! Either the island really *is* haunted or . . .'

The Sergeant looked at him anxiously; the boy's mind must be affected, he told himself uneasily. 'Haunted?' he repeated, puzzled. 'The island haunted?'

Nick's brain felt like cotton-wool; he couldn't think straight. 'Either it's haunted or . . .'

The Sergeant stared at him. He'd suddenly remembered the feeling he'd had of a presence at the ruined cottage . . . of someone watching him. 'Have you been on the island this afternoon?' he asked quickly.

Nick shook his head.

'Are you certain?'

'I d-didn't land! I-I s-saw something, though! If it isn't ghosts . . . then what is it?'

It seemed like a good question to Perkins. 'What did you see, lad?' he asked eagerly. 'What makes you think the island's haunted?'

Nick started to talk then; the words came tumbling out in an incoherent jumble but the Sergeant got the gist of it. He began with the evening he had swum out to the island and finished up with the events of the afternoon. He told how nobody believed him, how everyone had laughed at him; he poured it all out into Perkins' strangely receptive ears; even about his meetings with Chris at the camp-site and elsewhere. He kept nothing back and at the end of his recital he slumped wearily down in his seat and waited for the latter's snort of disbelief.

To his surprise it didn't come! The Sergeant had heard him out with flatteringly close attention. He had even produced a note-book and pencil, sitting at the table and scribbling furiously. He asked a few questions at the end and carefully recorded Nick's answers.

'If it isn't a ghost, Sir, then what is it?' Nick said again in a weary voice.

'A good question, son!' murmured Perkins. 'Can you describe – er – Chris?'

'Tall, thin, thickish blond hair!'

'Hm!' There was a gleam of excitement in Perkins' eyes. 'Don't trouble your head any more about it. Leave it to us. We'll sort it out!'

Nick rubbed his forehead; he wondered whether he was going out of his mind. 'Sort *what* out?' he asked dully.

'Don't bother about it!' Perkins repeated. 'Tell you another time . . . Now I'm getting us both a cup of tea and a scrambled egg or something. I'm sure your aunt won't mind!'

He put the kettle on and went to the fridge. As he did so Nick came back to reality; a frightened look spread over his face. 'What's Uncle Bob going to say?' he murmured fearfully.

The Sergeant's expression changed; he shook his head and looked serious. 'Ah, that's another matter altogether, I'm afraid!'

'I've explained why I had to do it . . . I was a laughing stock!' Nick said desperately.

'I appreciate that! It was stupid, all the same – taking things into your own hands and risking your life, not to mention other people's! Still, you weren't to know!' he added mysteriously.

'Know what?' Nick asked vaguely but the Sergeant, busy buttering toast, didn't answer. He handed Nick a mug of steaming chocolate.

'I'll be round to see you again tomorrow for a few more details if you're feeling up to it.' He looked at the boy more closely; he was flushed as though he had a high temperature, which wasn't surprising . . . He ought to be tucked up in bed with a hot water bottle by now, he told himself, otherwise he'd develop pneumonia! Where had the MacLarens got to? he wondered.

The next moment voices wafted in from the garden, the front door opened and steps sounded in the hall. Bob and Jane MacLaren, Tessa and Meg burst into the kitchen, and a look of relief leapt into their eyes as they saw Nick slouched in the chair. He was obviously in a bit of a state, though! What had he been up to now? they wondered, and looked enquiringly at Perkins.

'A hot bath then straight to bed seems to be the order of the day for this young man,' the Sergeant said. 'Nick here's suffering from exposure and exhaustion.'

'What's happened?' Bob MacLaren asked abruptly. 'We've been searching for two hours or more!'

'Tell you later!' muttered Perkins, and the girls glanced at one another. *Now* what had he been doing? they asked themselves.

Mrs MacLaren looked at her nephew. 'Off to bed then, Nick!' she ordered. 'Could you fill a hot water bottle please, girls!'

They nodded, and she steered her nephew out of the

room. He was in no state to talk, as she soon discovered. He appeared so feverish, in fact, that she telephoned the doctor when he was safely tucked up in bed. Having done that she went downstairs to the kitchen again.

Sergeant Perkins was still there, talking to her husband, Tessa and Meg. The twins were there, too; they had been next door all afternoon. Everybody was looking stunned, she saw with alarm, and Tessa and Meg seemed near to tears. The Sergeant went all over the horrific details of the rescue operation again for her benefit. Then, having supplied her with certain other information which he had already given to the others, he departed, promising to come again the next day.

The doctor called later, and not a moment too soon. By that time Nick's condition had deteriorated; he had slipped into a state of semi-consciousness and was rambling. Forty-eight hours complete rest was prescribed and Dr Jones said he would call first thing in the morning, or earlier, if required.

Four very subdued children sat down to supper later that evening. Apart from the horrific events of the afternoon, Sergeant Perkins had disclosed details of a bank robber on the run, armed and dangerous, believed to be in hiding in the area. Nick had certainly behaved very irresponsibly once again, taking old Bill's boat without permission and going off to the island under such conditions. Yet the MacLarens and his sister couldn't help but feel he'd had some slight justification! For after what Sergeant Perkins had divulged about the bank robber, they thought they understood everything now . . .

It didn't make them feel any better to learn what Nick had told the Sergeant. He had taken the rowing-boat and gone out to the island in a last desperate attempt to prove to his cousins and his sister that he wasn't as stupid as they all thought he was!

Well, he didn't need to prove his point now, did he? It was all too abundantly clear!

Why had the policeman been so interested in Chris from

the camp-site, though? they asked themselves uneasily. Sergeant Perkins hadn't actually said anything, he had merely stated that he would be helping them with their enquiries. That was enough, though, surely; everybody knew what that meant. The thought filled them all with total horror and disbelief!

Chris – a dangerous bank robber; it was hard to credit. Admittedly they hadn't seen all that much of him; he had kept himself very much to himself and had joined in the club activities only now and again. All the same, it was the very last thing anyone would have connected him with.

Bob MacLaren shook his head and looked grave. 'I'm afraid one can't always go by appearances,' he told them sadly. 'Still, we must wait and see, and hope for the best. Perhaps it isn't as bad as it sounds!'

With Nick quite seriously ill and Chris under a cloud, Tessa and Meg couldn't settle to anything for the remainder of the evening. They were just thinking about going to bed when there came an urgent ringing at the front door-bell.

'Who's that?' Meg asked gloomily.

'I don't know,' Tessa shrugged. 'I'll go and see.'

Chapter 15

Chris Explains

Tessa caught her breath when she saw who was standing on the doorstep. Their visitor's face was ashen, his hair plastered to his head; a torn shirt and muddied jeans completed the picture. Chris was the very last person she had expected to see, and a small shiver of fear ran down her spine. Was he armed? she asked herself; and glanced quickly round at Meg standing behind her. What should they do? Shut the door on him, lock him in her father's office whilst they rang the police, or what?

'I-is your . . . f-father in, Tessa? I-I need to speak to him, i-it's urgent!' Chris's voice came in choking gasps, he looked all in. His gaze travelled beyond Tessa to Meg and he added breathlessly, 'I-is Nick . . . ?' and seemed unable to go on.

'He's home and, er . . . well, not too good at the moment!' Tessa said. From what Sergeant Perkins had told them about Chris's playing at ghosts again, they were not surprised he was worried.

'He'll be OK in a few days, though!' Meg added.

Chris relaxed visibly; a load seemed to have been taken off his mind. 'Could . . . could I see your father, please?' he asked again.

'Er . . . yes, right, come in!' In spite of what the Sergeant had said, Tessa found it difficult to believe that such a decent, straightforward-looking guy as Chris could be guilty of such a crime. As for Meg, she felt devastated. There just had to be some logical explanation, she told herself; she just couldn't accept that a fellow-member of the youth club and someone who professed to be a Christian into the bargain, could be a dangerous bank robber. Yet how could one be sure? She bit her lip as she thought of her uncle's words, 'You can't always go by appearances!'

Both girls were hugely relieved, therefore, when they heard footsteps coming along the passage and Bob MacLaren appeared.

'Chris to see you, Dad!' Tessa murmured, and he stopped short, taken by surprise. He soon recovered himself, however, and subjected their visitor to a quick, searching scrutiny. The boy was near the end of his tether, that much was obvious. There was no doubt about it; he certainly resembled the man Perkins had described to them – tall, lean, with thick blond hair! Bob MacLaren sighed, for in the short time he had known the lad from the camp-site, he had formed quite a high opinion of him. Why had he come here? he asked himself; to spin a yarn, or to own up and seek advice? He ran a quick eye over him and decided it was unlikely he had a gun hidden away. As far as looks went he appeared perfectly honest and straighforward; but then, as he had just told the girls, one never could tell . . .

Chris seemed to read his thoughts. 'It's all right, Sir!' he said quietly. 'I-I'm not armed and I'm not a bank robber! I-I . . .' and all three of them thought he was about to faint.

'Come into the office!' Bob MacLaren invited, for something in the way the boy had spoken rang true. 'We won't be disturbed there.' He looked meaningly at Tessa and Meg and they moved reluctantly towards the front door. Their visitor intervened, however.

'Please let them stay, Mr MacLaren! I'd like them to hear, too!'

'Right then!' he agreed and Tessa looked at Meg and smiled as her father led the way into a small room off the hall. 'Find yourselves seats!' he said, and the girls perched themselves on the desk, whilst Chris sat opposite them on a high stool.

'OK then – fire away!' Bob MacLaren told him, and Chris took a deep, steadying breath.

'I haven't done anything criminal, Sir, really I haven't!' he began. 'It's all an awful misunderstanding . . . I-I thought at first they were after me because I'd been going to the island and I took fright and ran and . . .'

'Steady on now, lad! The police were after you and you thought . . . ?' Bob MacLaren interrupted.

'I thought they were chasing me because I was trespassing . . .'

'Trespassing? On the island! Anyone can go on the island, you know!'

'Yes, but – well, I've been going over there quite a lot lately!' He glanced at Tessa and Meg who were both holding their breath. 'Then just now, on my way here, I read the headlines on somebody's newspaper and I guessed what the police are thinking . . . ! They've got it all wrong though, Sir, but I'm afraid they'll never believe me! . . . Perhaps I'd better start from the beginning . . .'

'A good idea, son, take your time . . . First of all, though, I think we could all do with something to drink.' He looked at the girls who took the hint and jumped up.

'Don't let him start until we get back!' Tessa pleaded as they left the room.

'All right! Be quick, though!'

So Chris waited until they returned with mugs of cocoa and biscuits on a tray. He took his gratefully and after a few sips went on, 'I left school at the end of the summer term. I was fortunate enough to be offered a job almost straight away – just the sort of job I'd hoped for. I wasn't due to start until September so I decided to come down here camping!'

Bob MacLaren was listening intently. 'What sort of a job, Chris?' he asked.

'In a publishing office. I want to be a writer,' he admitted a shade apologetically. 'As a matter of fact I'm writing a book. That's why I've been going over to the island. I wanted somewhere I could write and take photographs without being disturbed.'

Tessa's eyes lit up with sudden comprehension; a smile spread over her face. 'I see!' she said excitedly. 'So it was *you*, was it?'

Meg was thinking hard. 'I think I see, too,' she murmured, beginning to chuckle. 'At least some of it, anyway!'

'Yes, I'm afraid it was! I thought it would be a nice quiet place to write and take photographs . . .'

Tessa was looking intrigued. 'What sort of a book?' she asked.

'On natural history – birds and plants and things.'

Meg forgot everything else in her excitement. 'How absolutely super!' she exclaimed. 'Can I have a signed copy when it's published?'

'Don't interrupt, girls! Let him have his say!' Bob MacLaren put in. 'So you thought the island would be a good place to write, Chris? . . . And so it would have been, I suppose,' he added with a wry smile, 'had not my nephew fancied himself as an Olympic swimmer!'

'Or an amateur detective!' Tessa added, with a giggle.

'I sort of got the idea Nick was interested in the island, too,' Chris went on. 'He was on the cliff one evening soon after I started going over there. I'd just come up from Sandy Bay where I leave my boat in a cave. He was standing looking out to sea . . .'

'That must have been the first evening of the holiday!' Tessa interrupted. 'You're right, Chris, Nick was absolutely mad keen on the island right from the beginning . . . he was besotted with it!'

'He came along to the camp-site with the twins – the next morning, I think it was – and they were talking about it. Stupid, I know, but I got the idea that Nick knew about me going over there . . . My guilty conscience, I suppose!'

'We all make mistakes sometimes,' Bob MacLaren said.

'Anyway, when he turned up that night – goodness

knows how he didn't get drowned – I was convinced he was snooping on me.'

The girls were all ears now. 'Nick's ghost!' Tessa said, beginning to laugh again.

'Why did he think you were a ghost?' Meg asked puzzled.

'Well, you see, I often went over after dark and stayed a couple of days. That's why I couldn't get to the club meetings as much as I would have liked. I took my sleeping-bag and a . . . sheet!'

There was a slight pause.

'A *white* sheet!' Tessa burst in as inspiration dawned. 'Poor old Nick, he wasn't as daft as we thought he was, was he?' and she started to laugh.

'He deserved all he got, all the same!' Bob MacLaren said severely.

'I did it on the spur of the moment. I thought it would frighten him off . . .' Chris explained.

'It certainly did that!' Meg said with a snort.

'I didn't clout him one, though!' Chris added hastily. 'I gathered that that was what he had been saying! He looked shattered when he saw me and stepped back so suddenly he must have tripped or something. I missed that bit, though; I just grabbed my things and made tracks for the boat!'

Bob MacLaren smiled. 'It makes sense!' he said, then his expression changed. 'I'm afraid my nephew's nosiness and sense of the dramatic have landed him up in even worse trouble this afternoon!'

'I was coming to that!' Chris said quickly. 'I was on the island when the storm blew up, sheltering in the cottage. I was looking out of one of the windows when a rowing-boat appeared offshore; it was trying to land and I guessed it was Nick. I ran down the beach signalling that I was coming to his rescue but there was a weird aura over everything and what with that and the lightning flashing around, he must have thought I was the ghost! He started rowing out to sea again; it was crazy! He was heading straight out towards the reef!'

'Yes, we know the rest all right – only too well!' Bob MacLaren looked grim. 'He's lucky to be alive. We'll tell you about the rescue another time.'

'It wasn't your fault anyway, Chris!' Meg said.

'Nobody could blame you for that!' Tessa added. 'It was just unfortunate.'

'I watched him disappear into the mist,' Chris went on, 'then I tried to launch my boat and go after him. It was impossible, though, it would have been suicidal! So I decided to get away from the island as soon as the storm blew over and raise the alarm. I kept looking out for him, but there was thick fog everywhere and soon after I thought I saw someone over by the cottage. I wondered whether it was Nick by some strange chance, but when I got there whoever it was had gone.'

He stopped for a breather, then went on. 'When the storm had blown over I discovered that my boat was practically waterlogged. It took me a while to bale the water out and I was just about to set off when I saw three men by the cottage. I soon realised it was the police and I went over and started trying to tell them about Nick. They wouldn't listen, though; said I was to go along with them to the police station to help them with their enquiries. I panicked and started to run. It was stupid, I know, but what with one thing and another . . .' He showed signs of breaking down at this point.

'Take it easy, lad!' Bob MacLaren advised.

'I went to the boat and they went off – to theirs presumably. I've just had an outboard motor fitted and I got away quickly. They followed me all the way over but I'd got a start on them. I hid in the sand-dunes and they started looking all over the beach. I made a dash for it and on the way here I saw the newspaper headlines and realised then what was up! I decided to come along here and explain it all to you. Why should they be after *me*, Mr MacLaren?'

'I'm afraid you've got young Nick to thank for this,'

Bob MacLaren explained. 'He told Sergeant Perkins after he'd been rescued that he thought you were up to something or other over on the island. You strongly resemble the bank raider, it seems, and they came to the wrong conclusion. You did the right thing anyway, coming here.'

'Phew, I see!' Chris was silent for a moment, thinking. 'Running away was the wrong thing to do, I suppose.'

Bob MacLaren shook his head. 'It was understandable! . . . Well, well, what a story!' he murmured.

'*You* all believe me, though, don't you?' Chris asked anxiously, looking from one to the other.

'Of course we do!' they told him in chorus.

'How on earth am I to convince the police though?' He searched in his pockets and brought out a small note-book. 'There are some of my notes,' he said, 'and I've got lots more at the camp-site. Unfortunately I left some over on the island, too, in my hurry!'

'They'll be safe enough there, old chap, don't worry!' Bob MacLaren got to his feet. 'Now I think we'd better get along to the police station. They know what you look like now and they'll be scouring the neighbourhood!'

Chris got up reluctantly, pulling a face.

'All you have to do is tell them what you've told us,' Meg said encouragingly.

'I only hope it will be as simple as that!' he murmured. 'I hope Nick will be all right,' he added anxiously.

'Nick's got youth and strength on his side! He'll be up and about in a few days, no doubt,' Bob MacLaren said as they went out of the front door. 'Explain everything to Mother, won't you, girls? Tell here where I've gone and that I'll be back as soon as we've got Chris sorted out. I expect she's still with Nick.'

Tessa and Meg promised they would and accompanied them both down to the gate.

'What a story we'll have to tell Melanie tomorrow!' Meg said as they watched her uncle and Chris walk quickly away down the road.

Chapter 16

The End of It All

The next few days were critical ones for Nick. The doctor's forty-eight hours turned out to be an optimistic assessment of the situation. Pneumonia had set in and Nick tossed, delirious, for nearly a week. From the way he rambled on it was obvious he was reliving his ghastly experience in his dreams. He gradually got back to normal, however, and was soon lying out in the garden on a sun-lounger, recuperating. Chris was his first visitor; Nick literally sat up and blinked when he saw him.

Chris greeted him with a cheerful grin. He was much relieved to see Nick well on the way to recovery – for in some measure he felt that what had happened had been partly his fault. 'Hi there!' he said. 'Feeling better then?'

Nick looked puzzled. 'I thought . . .' he began.

'You thought I'd be behind bars by now, I suppose,' Chris said dryly. 'I want to apologise for all the confusion.'

Nick looked embarrassed; things were beginning to come back. 'What's been going on?' he asked.

'The police found the bank robber early this morning – further down the coast.'

Nick's eyes widened.

'Bank robber!' he murmured.

'You probably didn't know,' Chris explained, 'but they were looking for a dangerous bank robber.'

Nick rubbed his forehead confusedly. 'I thought . . .' he began again; then petered out, at a loss as to how to go on.

Chris looked amused. 'You thought I was the bank robber, I suppose!' he finished for him.

'N-not exactly! I – I didn't know about a bank robber!' A sudden idea came to Nick and his eyes widened. 'I say,' he said, 'was it the bank robber who was playing at ghosts on the island, then?'

'No, that was me! The first time, at any rate. I didn't bash you one, though – you fell! Sorry about that, too, by the way. The second time I wasn't playing at ghosts at all; I was only trying to . . . Anyway, don't worry about it!' he finished, for Nick was looking really bewildered by now.

Melanie turned up at that moment, followed by Badger. The collie thrust a cold nose into Nick's hot hand.

'Two more visitors for you!' said Chris.

'Hello, Nick!' Melanie said. 'Glad you're better!'

'Hello, Melanie! Smashing to see you! . . . Hello, Badger!'

Tessa, Meg and the twins came out on to the lawn then and joined them.

'I was telling Nick about the bank robber!' Chris said.

Nick looked at Chris; he still couldn't quite sort it out, it was all very puzzling! 'What were you doing on the island?' he asked curiously.

'Chris is writing a book!' Meg explained.

'A book! What's that got to do with him being on the island?'

'That's why he went over there, don't you see?' Tessa said. 'To write his book! . . . It's hard work writing a book; you need to get away somewhere where it's quiet and you won't be disturbed!'

Nick looked disappointed. 'Was that all?' he said; it sounded tame, somehow – not a bit what he'd thought! He'd wasted an awful lot of time and energy and got himself into frightful trouble all for nothing, apparently! All the same he was glad Chris wasn't being detained at Her Majesty's pleasure! It was decent of him to have taken the trouble to come and see him, particularly after the way he'd suspected him! He probably wasn't a bad bloke when you got to know him.

'So that was all you were doing on the island, then?' Nick said thoughtfully.

'Sorry to disappoint you!' Chris laughed.

Tessa looked towards the house as that moment. 'Here's Mum with iced drinks and strawberries and cream!' she announced.

'And here are two more visitors for you!' Meg said as David came through the gate with Sheba.

'You're just in time!' Tessa called out.

'Hi Nick!' David greeted. 'Nice to see you up again!'

They all spread out on the grass in the hot sunshine and Nick looked at each in turn. He didn't know whether this little gathering had been pre-arranged but it was jolly good of them to have come; they were quite a decent lot after all, he told himself! He attacked his strawberries with relish, glad to find that his appetite was returning.

Uncle Bob turned up then. 'We're all going over to the island again on Saturday afternoon!' he said and looked at Nick. 'The doctor thinks you should be fit enough to come too by then,' he told his nephew. 'If you want to, that is!'

'Hope you will!' Melanie said.

'Chris has almost finished his book now,' Meg laughed, 'so we won't be disturbing him!'

'Great!' Nick said. After all that had happened to him, the idea of going with the youth club didn't seem too terrible. He started thinking about the island again; even if it had lost some of its appeal after what he'd just learnt, it would be fun to go over there again.

'It's been specially arranged for your benefit,' Meg told him. 'To celebrate your getting better!'

'Have I been awfully ill then?' he asked, wrinkling his forehead.

'Quite ill,' Tessa said. 'You were rambling some of the time!' She remembered how worried she and Meg had been. Their efforts to patch things up at the end of the picnic had turned out to be too late and had Nick not recovered they would have felt themselves partly to blame. He'd got to learn the hard way, though, her father had told them; perhaps now he would come to his senses!

Meg looked at Nick and started to laugh. 'One day you were out rowing with a ghost which dropped you off on a rock and left you there for the night!' she remembered. 'Another time you were helping the police track down a dangerous criminal by the name of Chris!'

Everybody collapsed with laughing at that, including Nick!

*　　*　　*

Saturday turned out to be another glorious day. They left the harbour around ten; most of the youth club had turned up. Gary Travers was there looking rather subdued; he was glad to see Nick up and about again; he felt a bit guilty about what had happened, too. For that matter, so did the twins! They made a point of sharing their sticky sweets with their cousin on the way over.

Leaning over the side of *Golden Spray* next to Nick, Meg thought of the last time they had made the crossing. A lot had happened since then and she felt a different person – more self-reliant, no longer so easily led. Later in the day, Nick and Melanie made their way to the ruined cottage. Meg was there with Chris who was taking close-ups of wild flowers. Tessa and David turned up presently and the six friends climbed the stone steps to the level of the upstairs room and wandered around the outside. The place no longer held any terrors for Meg, and as for Nick, it was nothing more exciting now than a derelict old building – fascinating all the same. He looked at the pile of ashes in the corner and Chris followed his gaze.

'Gets a bit chilly out here at nights!' Chris grinned, reading his thoughts.

Melanie remembered the piece of paper she and Nick had found.

'You should be more careful to cover your tracks, Chris!' she laughed. 'You left a page of your book under that stone!'

At that moment a horrendous shriek rent the stillness. Melanie went outside and looked up at the chimney-pot. It was the greater black-backed gull, and Nick caught Melanie's eye and grinned.

'That a friend of yours, Chris?' Melanie asked.

'He's a fine specimen!' Chris said.

The time sped by; they explored the rest of the island, swam, and played beach games. Finally there was the epilogue. Steve was talking about making decisions.

'We all have to make decisions as we go through life,' he said. 'Many of you will have big decisions to make soon – what to do when you leave school . . . ' Nick looked at Chris sitting further down the row. No problem for him there – maybe he'd be a famous writer one day, make a name for himself! Not my sort of thing at all, thought Nick, but all right for those who like it.

There was Dave too – all set to follow in his father's footsteps at the coastguard station, guarding Britain's coastline. As for himself, Nick had no idea what he wanted to do – except that it had to be something different, something exciting! His love of adventure had landed him up in an awful lot of trouble so far, though . . .

'Is it a life of adventure you're looking for?' Steve asked, and Nick glanced up quickly. He had thought for the moment that Steve was speaking directly to him . . . 'If so, why not channel your love of excitement and adventure into worthwhile service for Christ?' He went on to outline opportunities at home and abroad – working with the underprivileged in the third world, with the starving in refugee camps and in war-torn areas of the world . . .

Nick's attention became held and riveted. His mind went back to the evening of the barbecue. Steve had been talking along the same lines on that occasion – giving one's life over to God . . . He hadn't listened then, hadn't accepted the challenge . . .

It came to the final prayer and Nick made up his mind. He'd been though a traumatic experience, been near to death. God hadn't sent a whale but he'd sent Sergeant Perkins and the other policemen! Nick had thanked the Sergeant for his part in the rescue operation when he'd called round at the guest-house earlier that morning, said how sorry he was for the trouble he'd caused. He'd already apologised to his uncle and aunt and on his uncle's instructions he'd penned a note to old Bill asking his forgiveness for taking his boat.

Now he needed to ask God's forgiveness. It came to the final prayer and Nick bowed his head, dedicating his life to the service of Christ and his fellow men.

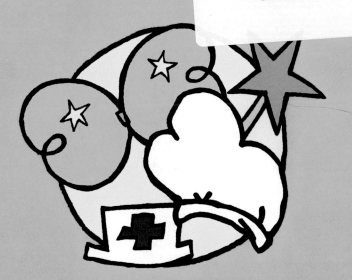

Collect 5 tokens and get a free poster!*

All you have to do is collect five funky tokens!

You can snip one from any of these cool Bang on the Door books!

0 00 715297 3

0 00 715309 0

0 00 715307 4

0 00 715308 2

0 00 715305 8

**Send 5 tokens with a completed coupon
to: Bang on the Door Poster Offer**

PO Box 142, Horsham, RH13 5FJ (UK residents)

c/- HarperCollins Publishers (NZ) Ltd,
PO Box 1, Auckland (NZ residents)

c/- HarperCollins Publishers, PO Box 321,
Pymble NSW 2073, Australia
(for Australian residents)

0 00 715306 6

Title: Mr ☒ Mrs ☐ Miss ☐ Ms ☒ First name: .... Surname: ....

Address: ....

....

....

Postcode: .... Child's date of birth: ...... / ...... /

email address: ....

Signature of parent/guardian: ....

Tick here if you do not wish to receive further information about children's books ☐

(LSO)

1 token

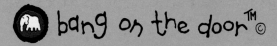

bang on the door™©

little sweetheart dresses up

Collins

An imprint of HarperCollinsPublishers

Little sweetheart was going to play her favourite game in the whole world. She loved it more than fluffy pink marshmallows, blowing bubbles and even more than bouncing on her trampoline.

Can you guess what it was?

Dressing up!

"What shall I wear today?"
little sweetheart
thought.

"My nurse's uniform?

Or perhaps
my fairy wings?

Maybe my
ballerina shoes?

Or my bride's veil?

Or even my
chef's hat?"

shoes

"I know!" thought
little sweetheart.
"I'm going to be
someone very special.

bag

hat

"Gorgeous!" said **little**
sweetheart as she admired
her outfit in the mirror.
"These sparkly jewels look
fabulous, but there seems
to be something missing...
I wonder what it could be?"

She searched through her dressing up box...

to find something else to match her outfit...

but nothing
she tried...

seemed
quite right.

Little sweetheart was starting to
feel glum when she heard the
doorbell ring.

ding – dong

It was her friend,
little princess. "Come in,"
said little sweetheart.
"I'm having lots of
fun dressing up!"

"No," replied her friend,
"Give me a clue!"

"Okay then," laughed
little sweetheart.
"I live in a castle and
I'm very important!"

"Oh! Now I know!"
giggled **little princess.**

"You're a princess, of course!
But you've forgotten one
very special finishing touch."
She delicately put her crown
on little sweetheart's head.

"Oh!" gasped **little sweetheart**.
"But I can't wear your crown."

"Don't worry silly, I always
keep a spare in my bag in
case of an emergency,"
laughed **little princess**.

"That's perfect!"
said **little sweetheart.**
"Now you look just like me!"

"No," smiled **little princess,**
"You look just like me!"

First published in Great Britain by HarperCollins Publishers Ltd in 2003

1 3 5 7 9 10 8 6 4 2

ISBN: 0-00-715308-2

Bang on the door character copyright:

© 2003 Bang on the Door all rights reserved.

bang on the door® is a trademark

Exclusive right to license by Santoro

www.bangonthedoor.com

Text © 2003 HarperCollins Publishers Ltd.

A CIP catalogue record for this title is available from the British Library.

The HarperCollins website address is: www.fireandwater.com

Printed and bound in Hong Kong